EDGE

Edge's wanderings had become aimless again, and he rode a more bitter and brutal trail than ever, seeking only to stay alive. He lived for the sheer cold-blooded pleasure of making his enemies pay for the suffering he had been caused. He didn't question himself or his actions. He simply rode the trail. And sometimes he arrived in towns like Seascape—just in time for a carnival of gold and death.

EDGE by George G. Gilman

#5 BLOOD ON SILVER   (17-225, $3.50)
The Comstock Lode was one of the richest silver strikes the world had ever seen. So Edge was there. So was the Tabor gang—sadistic killers led by a renegade Quaker. The voluptuous Adele Firman, a band of brutal Shoshone Indians, and an African giant were there, too. Too bad. They learned that gold may be warm but silver is death. They didn't live to forget Edge.

#6 RED RIVER   (17-226, $3.50)
In jail for a killing he didn't commit, Edge is puzzled by the prisoner in the next cell. Where had they met before? Was it at Shiloh, or in the horror of Andersonville?

This is the sequel to KILLER'S BREED, an earlier volume in this series. We revisit the bloody days of the Civil War and incredible scenes of cruelty and violence as our young nation splits wide open, blue armies versus gray armies, tainting the land with a river of blood. And Edge was there.

Available wherever paperbacks are sold, or order direct from the Publisher. Send cover price plus 50¢ per copy for mailing and handling to Pinnacle Books, Dept.17-331, 475 Park Avenue South, New York, N.Y. 10016. Residents of New York, New Jersey and Pennsylvania must include sales tax. DO NOT SEND CASH.

EDGE

TIGER'S GOLD

by
George G. Gilman

PINNACLE BOOKS
WINDSOR PUBLISHING CORP.

PINNACLE BOOKS

are published by

Windsor Publishing Corp.
475 Park Avenue South
New York, NY 10016

Eighth printing: April, 1990

Printed in the United States of America

for
J. A.
who adds it up

CHAPTER ONE

"Hey, mister! You wanna see me throw knives at this pretty little girl?"

The knife-thrower was doing his own spieling and he wasn't too successful at it. He was almost naked, dressed only in a stained and dirty loincloth knotted at his bulging belly. But he sweated a lot, from the blazing sun of noon and the effort of attracting the crowd to go into his tent and see his entertainment. Sweated so much that the brown dye coating his thin face and stockily built, flaccid body was streaked pale in a lot of places where the salty moisture had trickled down the flesh. One potential viewer of the show waited before the wooden platform set up in front of the elongated wedge tent. He was a scrawny boy of about fifteen with hungry eyes which stared unblinkingly out of a face made ugly by massed groups of ugly red and yellow pustules. The fingers of one hand constantly explored the poisoned swellings on his face

1

while his other hand moved rhythmically in a pocket of his patched levis.

"What'd she do to deserve that?" the tall man astride the big black stallion asked wryly. He eyed the girl with cool appraisal.

She was about twenty, which was half the age of the man who shared the platform with her, and at six feet she stood a head taller than he. A blue-eyed blonde, her face had a certain shallow prettiness. Her body was a little too full-blown but her legs were good—long and slender. Her clothing was scanty. A short-length, brightly colored tunic of red and blue, cut low to swell her breasts above the neckline; and black net hose. The hose had been repaired with various shades of yarn in several places.

A sign over the entrance of the tent proclaimed her name as Jo Jo Lamont. Her partner was billed as Eagle-eyed Turk.

Turk swiped away a runnel of sweat from his brow before it could course into his eye. Anger twisted his thin mouthline. "Jokes I don't need," he growled. "Not in this heat with business this bad."

"Things are tough all round," the tall man answered, licking trail dust from his lips.

Jo Jo Lamont had thrust out her breasts and spread a bright smile across her face when the man halted his horse. Now that it was obvious he had no intention of becoming a paying customer, her body took on a weary sag and she stared malevolently at the horny teenager.

"You got the five cents admission money, sonny?" she demanded harshly.

"Ain't got nothin'," the boy told her dully, eyes raking her legs and body as his hands maintained their constant busy movements.

2

"So butt out!" the girl snarled. "This ain't no free peep show!"

She leaned forward as she spoke, her prettiness suffering under the hardening lines of anger. The boy took a step backwards, a broad grin creasing his pustulous features as his avid eyes captured a long-awaited view down Jo Jo's deep cleavage.

"Didn't cost me nothin', lady!" he taunted in delight, then whirled around and sprinted along the carny's midway.

"And how about you, mister?" Jo Jo demanded. "You just hanging around for a free show?"

Her anger was still high, her cheeks flushed a deeper red than the rouge which decorated them. The dye-run face of her partner showed dejection.

"Just looking for a job is all, ma'am." The tall man touched his heels against the flanks of the horse. "But even if you were paying, you've got nothing that interests me."

"Turk!" Jo Jo shrieked. "You hear what that saddletramp said to me?"

"Yeah, I heard," Turk said tensely. Then he raised his voice. "Roll up, folks! Roll up and see the beautiful Jo Jo Lamont dice with sudden death. See the flashing knife blades and watch them sink into the wood a hairsbreadth from the frail flesh of this lovely young girl."

He was talking to the hot air, for with the boy and the rider gone there was nobody to hear him. His tent was set up in a bad position, but that wasn't the only reason why business was slow. All of the spielers fronting the sideshows on the midway, even those close to town, were shouting themselves hoarse to no avail.

Riding unhurriedly down the midway, which was in fact the final stretch of trail leading into the eastern

3

end of Seascape, Oregon, the tall man astride the black stallion was barraged with competing voices. Invitations, challenges, urgings and pleadings were hurled against his inattentive ears by spielers fronting a dozen different kinds of shows. Vividly lettered signs, many showing pictorial exaggerations, decorated the tents to back up the verbal exhortations.

Among the attractions was an Oriental fire-eater who doubled with an exotic dancer; an acrobatic clown; a dark-skinned animal trainer with two tigers; a fortune-teller; a fat lady; a bearded lady; and a rubber man.

The tall man rode impassively past all of these and there was just the merest flicker of interest in his eyes as he approached the tent which had been pitched in the very best position, immediately at the end of Seascape's main street. This was the show that had cornered all the business. Despite the fact that it had no front man to drum up custom. Instead there was a quartet of bulky-bodied, hard-eyed men: two each side of the tent entrance through which a long line of paying customers were shuffling. Another man—slight of stature, pale of face and dressed like an Eastern dude—sat behind a small table set up in the tent entrance. There was a tin box on the table and into this he dropped the money paid over by each eager customer.

The sign above the entrance was simply a plain wooden plank crudely painted with black lettering: *SEE THE BIG GOLD WORTH $1,000,000. 50 cents men, women and children.*

The tall man halted his horse opposite the tent entrance and took out the makings of a cigarette from the pocket of his sweat-stained, dusty shirt. The four guards flanking the man taking the money worked the actions of the winchesters canted across

4

the fronts of their bodies. Their eyes raked the rider
in a cool, fast appraisal.

"You wanna see the big gold, join the end of the
line," the eldest of the guards growled. "Otherwise,
move outta the way."

The tall man concentrated upon rolling the cigarette, sticking down the paper and then hanging it at
the corner of his mouth to light it. Only then did he
give any sign of having heard what was said to him.
With a steady, blank-eyed gaze, he looked at each of
the four in turn. The one who had spoken was about
forty, with knotted muscles that bulged his shirt and
a prominent belly that looked soft. He had a smalled-
eyed, wide-mouthed, deeply-scored face. The other
three were all in their mid-twenties. They were
smooth-faced under their stubble. Their tall, wide
builds matched that of the eldest man, without the
soft gut.

"You own the trail, feller?" the rider asked.

The dude behind the table looked up. The line of
customers stopped shuffling forward. Everyone eyed
the rider. Expressions varied from arrogance on the
faces of the guards, through mild curiosity and irrita-
tion among the customers, to a hint of nervousness
on the countenance of the dude.

They saw a man in his thirties, but it was difficult
to tell how many years before he reached forty. A
man who was at least three inches taller than six feet
and maybe weighed two hundred pounds. A lot of
weight, but evenly distributed over a lean frame so
that, even while sitting easily in the saddle, there was
a suggestion he could move fast and with power. His
face was composed of features which were a mixture
of the Aryan and the Latin: light blue eyes, a hawkish
nose, high cheekbones, a narrow mouth and a firm
jaw. Spare features, with burnished, weathered skin

5

criss-crossed by the lines of suffering and framed by thick, jet black hair that fell to brush his shoulders. A half-breed, certainly, everybody decided. Whether handsome or ugly, it depended—upon how the beholder regarded the quality of harshness which had played a part in molding the man's appearance. Did it arouse sympathy because here was a man who had obviously undergone great hardship: or did it stir a degree of revulsion because in him was the capability to make others suffer as much as he had?

It took a second look at the man to decipher these alternative conclusions: and to meet his piercing, ice-cold gaze was to realize the truth. If evil and cruelty were ugly, then this man could become a walking nightmare.

"Me and my partners are paid to do a job," the eldest of the guards said flatly.

"A warning," the rider replied. "Don't point those guns at me—unless you intend to use them."

"Grainger!" the dude rasped. "We don't want trouble of our making."

Abruptly, there was renewed shuffling in the line. But in the opposite direction, as those close to the tent entrance backed away. The cries of the spielers had died away as soon as the rider had past by and halted before the crowd-pulling sideshow.

"Me and the boys are doin' our job, Mr. Case," Grainger answered. "I don't like the way he's lookin' the tent over."

"Looking's a habit with him! He done it to me back down the midway! Like I was some kind of prize steer or something!"

Turk and Jo Jo Lamont had called it a day. They had hauled the platform inside the tent, collected their knives, fastened the flap and were ambling wearily towards town. The girl's voice was strident with ill-tempered frustration. Her eyes were blazing as they met the steady gaze of the rider when he turned in the saddle.

"Saw enough to know you weren't a steer, ma'am," he said quietly, and his thin lips curled back to show his even teeth in a cold grin. "Close, but I'd say the resemblance was more to the udder sex."

"Turk!" Jo Jo screamed. "This drifter just called me a cow!"

The man was fast and he was accurate. Even when gripped by a sudden rage. He had not needed his partner's explanation. The dozen throwing knives were slotted into sheaths along a leather bandolier strung from his shoulder to waist. He had drawn one before Jo Jo screamed his name. And it was spinning through the hot air long before she translated the insult. But the tall man put his latent speed into lightning action. He crouched forward, against the neck of the stallion. The knife, aimed for a hit between the shoulder blades, sliced into the underside of his hat brim. It had enough power behind it to lift the hat from his head and scale it down into the dust of the midway.

The watchers held their collective breath. Except for Grainger and his three fellow guards. Used to sudden violence, they stood relaxed and grinning: waiting for the next move. But there was no fast follow-up to Turk's attack, nor a whiplash response from the rider.

"Christ, I could have killed him!" Turk said, aghast as he looked from his splayed throwing hand to where the low-crowned black hat lay with the knife blade piercing the brim. "My stinkin' temper!"

The rider's attitude became almost lazily slow again as he swung down from the saddle. Some sweat beads oozed up from the dirt-grimed pores of his forehead,

7

but that was the only change the close call with death had brought about in his appearance.

"Mister, am I glad you ducked!" Turk called, his voice shaking with emotion. Then he whirled towards Jo Jo. "One day I'm gonna hang on account of you!" he snarled.

"Kind of glad I ducked myself," the tall half-breed answered, flicking his cigarette out ahead of him and treading out its fire as he stooped to pick up the hat. His voice was as unassuming as his gait.

"Move back up again, folks!" Grainger yelled, his harsh tones shattering the final layer of lifting tension. "See the big gold worth a million bucks. It's gotta be better than watchin' a tough-talkin' saddletramp get cut down to size."

The slightly built, dude-dressed Case resumed his chore of collecting the admission money. But without the enthusiasm he had shown previously. A great deal of his attention was still on the tall half-breed. Not nervously, though. He was intrigued. The guards expressed taunting amusement.

The half-breed drew the knife from the brim and put the hat on his head without brushing off the dust. He ambled over to where the contrite-looking Turk stood beside the shocked Jo Jo. Now, the rouge stood out in garish contrast against her pallor.

"Gee, mister," she whispered, swallowing hard. "I didn't mean for him to try to kill you." She tried a smile and it looked a little sick. "Still no harm done, was there? No hard feelings?"

"Not against you," the tall man replied quietly. "But if you're that way inclined, the kid may still be feeling cocky."

Her jolted mind was still busy with the memory of the lightning knife attack. It took time for her to read the double-meaning into the words. And then there

8

was no time to scream at her partner. The half-breed smiled with his mouth at Turk and extended his right arm for a handshake. Turk was still staring at his own right hand, which had launched the knife. He looked up and saw the pleasant expression formed by the half-breed's mouth. It was impossible to see anything except a glittering blueness between the narrowed lids of the eyes.

The two men clasped hands.

"Glad you see it—"

The rest of the words were caught in Turk's throat. The grip of the long-fingered, brown-skinned hand of the half-breed was too hard. He applied strength far beyond that required for the mere firmness of friendship.

"Turk, don't trust!—" Jo Jo managed to shriek.

The warning came too late for her partner. But it did swing every eye on the midway towards the two men—just as the half-breed powered into a crouch and lunged his left arm up from his side. The speed he had showed in ducking under the lethal aim of the spinning knife now came into play again. In going down for the crouch, he also leaned backwards and jerked Turk towards him. The smaller man's natural instinct was to try to regain his balance as a cry of alarm ripped from his sweat-run lips. The action wrenched his arm ramrod stiff.

The knife was fisted in the half-breed's left hand. Sunlight glinted on the four inches of polished steel probing up from the encirclement of thumb and index finger. But only for an instant, as it swung in a blur of speed. The point dug into the scrawny flesh of Turk's armpit, on the outside of the humerus bone. It kept on going, slashing through muscle and tissue and veins, until it burst clear of the skin on the other side. Blood sprayed out ahead of the steel.

9

Turk screamed, the high-pitched sound swamping the gasps of horror which rippled through the crowd of watchers. And he continued to scream, coming close to soprano before his voice cracked. By then the knife had finished its slicing work. As soon as the point showed at the exit wound, the half-breed had drawn the knife towards him, along the arm. Spraying blood trailed its awesome course now: arcing into the dust as the finely honed metal slashed through the flesh from shoulder to elbow. There, it scraped against a knot of bone and glanced off course. It burst through a final layer of tissue and cut clear of the skin.

Pain, or perhaps the ghastly sight of his own mutilation, had already dropped the merciful blackness of unconsciousness over Turk's mind and he was starting to corkscrew to the ground. A long flap of blood-dripping flesh, broad at the shoulder and tapering to a point at the elbow, swung away from the parent arm. The half-breed released the limp hand of the terribly injured Turk and the man crumpled into a heap. The gruesome flap of skin and flesh exhausted its store of blood. But the long, meaty wound exposed by the slash continued to pump with sticky crimson. The thirsty ground sucked at it avidly. Flies swarmed in for a ravenous feast.

With the abrupt curtailment of the scream, a vast silence had clamped down over the carny. The droning of the hungry flies was eerily loud against the stillness. Massed shock seemed to have a physical presence, vibrating in the dry heat of the Oregon afternoon. Even Grainger and his three partners were shaken by the callous brutality of the lightning attack.

The half-breed was the first to move. The flick of his wrist was smooth and easy. But it sent the knife spinning with enough power to sink the blade through the flap of flesh and pin it to the ground. Then he did a slow pivot and ambled over to where the stallion stood, nostrils twitching at the scent of blood. Every man, woman and child on the midway followed his progress, with a single exception, their eyes expressed revulsion. Case, the dude, had recovered from his shock and watched the half-breed with excited interest as the tall man remounted his horse.

Jo Jo Lamont emitted a shuddering sob, then rushed to where Turk lay and fell to her knees beside him. But she couldn't look at the awesome wound. Still on her knees, she swung her body around to stare malevolently up at the mounted man.

"You stinking sonofabitch!" she shrieked at him. "Turk was my meal ticket. How's he gonna throw knives now?"

"He ain't," the half-breed told her quietly. "Especially not at me. That was the idea."

"What am I gonna do?" Jo Jo wailed, losing more of the watchers' sympathy with every word she uttered, stressing her own misfortune above Turk's suffering.

"Learn to chew over the crud before you spit it out. Maybe you'll find another guy to ride herd on you."

He heeled the horse into an easy walk, riding alongside the line of Seascape citizens waiting to see the big gold. The carny people from the other sideshows hurried forward to gather around the unconscious Turk and the sobbing Jo Jo.

"All he done was put a hole in your hat, mister!" a man in the line accused with heavy scorn. "Didn't have to do that to him."

The man's wife laid a restraining hand on his arm and trembled when the ice-blue, slitted eyes of the half-breed sought out the speaker.

"He hurt me, feller," the tall rider answered softly,

11

taking off his hat and brushing off the dust with a shirt sleeve. "Had to make him regret it."

The man in the crowd was short and fat—and brave. "Knife didn't even part your hair." He shook off his wife's hand angrily.

"Got me in a sensitive spot," the tall man said as he set the hat back on his head and rode past. "Hurt my dignity."

CHAPTER TWO

The half-breed, whose ethnic mix was the result of having a Scandinavian mother and a Mexican father, was named Edge. He had not been born with this name, but it served his purpose as well as the original. He had come by it at a time when the horrors and violence of war were behind him and a peaceful life as an Iowa wheat farmer should have been his. But fate had decreed this was not to be. It was almost as if God—or, more likely, Satan—had decided that Captain Josiah C. Hedges had learned the lessons of war too well for his knowledge and skills to be wasted.

For it was a chain of events outside his control, not a voluntary choice, that had driven him away from the end of the conflict between the North and the South and on to the start of a peacetime trail more bloody and vicious than anything he had experienced as a Union cavalry officer. Revenge had been the initial spur, driving him to seek retribution against the men who had destroyed everything he had fought

13

the war to preserve. Honor had been satisfied, but afterwards there had been no trail back into the kind of life that might have been.

Just a trail that went aimlessly forward, sometimes inviting and at other times compelling, the rootless man called Edge to follow it. Gaining and losing fortunes and in the process having to kill in order to survive. Killing fast and brutally, before he suffered the same fate. And to what end? Once he had succeeded in taking a tenuous grip on a future that was not aimless. But it had proved to be cruel fate playing a dirty trick. The hope of sharing a peaceful, happy life with a wife on a farm in the Dakotas had been more viciously shattered than the dream of returning home to Iowa and a kid brother.

Hatred and revenge had driven him out on to the trail again, but there was to be no honor satisfied this time. A lone man could not wipe out the entire Sioux nation, and what was the point: when the man discovered the bitter truth about the death of his wife? That he had contributed as much to her terrible end as the Indians.

And so the wanderings of Edge had become aimless again and he rode the trail more bitter and brutal than ever: seeking only to stay alive. Without reason. Unless it be to make all men pay for the suffering caused to him. Or for the sheer, cold-blooded pleasure he derived from responding to violence with a greater degree of violence? Perhaps because he did not want to know the answer, he never questioned himself or his actions. He simply rode the trail. Through the open country of the Mid and Far West most of the way. But sometimes arriving in towns like Seascape.

Allowing the stallion to make his own easy walking pace down the main street, Edge saw that he could go no further west on this course. For the town was set spectacularly atop high cliffs overlooking the vast, blue-green emptiness of the Pacific. But it did not make its living from the ocean. The sound of the breakers crashing against the base of the cliffs, distant but loud in their fury, provided audible evidence that the Pacific was too far below and too angry to accept boats. The great, broad belt of towering redwoods arcing around Seascape to the north, east and south and the strong scent of fresh sawdust permeated through the arid air witnessed this was a timber town.

It wasn't long since Edge had been in another town that drew its living from the massive forests of the north west. A town that had lived up to its ominous name of Hate. But he seldom reflected upon the past and as he angled his horse towards the front of the Redwood saloon he drove into the back of his mind the memories which the scent of sawdust threatened to stir. There was a drinking trough adjacent to the hitching rail and the stallion sucked thirstily at the sun-dappled water. It had been a long, hot ride for the sun had made its heat felt almost from the first moment it showed itself full-face above the horizon.

The shade of the covered sidewalk in front of the saloon was pleasant. Through the fastened opened batswings the air was even cooler. There was only one other person in the big room, and he wasn't large enough to give off much body heat. He was a short, skinny, middle-aged man with buck teeth and wire-framed eye-glasses. Standing behind the long, polished wood bar with a brass rail at its base, he wore a freshly-laundered white shirt and a much-stained leather apron. He showed more teeth in a wide grin of genuine pleasure as his only customer approached. He didn't seem to mind at all that Edge banged his hat against his black shirt and black levis, leaving a trail of dust on the previously clean floor.

"Welcome to you stranger!" he greeted effusively. "Seein' as how my regulars ain't in a drinkin' mood today, I'm buying the first one. For the pleasure of your company, like. Name your poison."

"Beer," Edge answered, leaning against the bar and hooking a heel over the rail. "On account of it's better than rye on a hot day and it's cheaper."

The grin stayed in place while the bartender drew the beer. "When Herb Alton stands treat in his own bar, you don't want to worry about the expense," he said happily.

Edge drew a handful of coins from his pants pocket and set them on the counter. "When I'm paying, I worry about the expense," he said. "And I'm paying."

"Suit yourself," Alton answered, deflated. He placed the foaming glass in front of the half-breed and slid five cents from the small pile of loose change.

"Usually do," Edge said.

The sound of Jo Jo's sobs, shuffling feet and low-voiced conversation drifted in from the street. Alton moved to the side to look around his customer as a group of the carny people moved along the street in front of the opened batswings. They were carrying Turk's inert form. The distraught Jo Jo trailed the group, ignored by them.

"What the hell happened?" Alton asked, more rhetorically than in expectation of an answer.

Edge was looking at a faded and curled notice pinned above the bottle-lined shelves behind the counter. It read: ROOMS TO RENT—50 CENTS A NIGHT. He glanced down at the coins and calculated there was forty cents in nickels and dimes. He raised the glass to his dusty lips. "Guy used his right arm

16

for the wrong thing," he muttered, and sank half the beer at a single swallow. It was cold and tasted better than anything he had ever swallowed before.

"Uh?" Alton asked, bewildered. "Looks to me like somebody got hurt." He craned his neck and went up on his toes to look through an end window in the saloon. "Yeah, they're goin' up to Doc Elkin's place." He shook his head ruefully and made tutting sounds. "I said all along them carny folk'd cause trouble. You see it, stranger?"

Edge was sipping the beer to extend his enjoyment of it. "Wasn't much to see. A woman opened her mouth and a guy got cut up over it."

"Mrs. Blackhouse was right!" Alton said with feeling. "Them there brazen females was sure to cause trouble. Flaunting their bodies on the open street like they was whores in a city cathouse."

Edge probed at the pile of change with a dirt-grimed finger. "How many hours will that buy me in one of your rooms?" he asked. "If I take a bath as well as rest up?"

Alton's generosity in offering to buy a drink was uncharacteristic. He eyed the pathetic heap of money with scorn and did a fast, long-range tally without having to touch the coins. "That forty cents'll buy you a room for as long as it takes you to have the bath."

Edge continued to sip his beer, but the direction of his hooded-eyed gaze drew the attention of the bartender to the notice above the shelves. Alton merely glanced at the curled sign. He shook his head.

"That rate applies when circumstances are normal, stranger. All the business premises in Seascape have upped their charges. On account of the carny people. It keeps them camped in the timber and outta town most of the time. It was Mrs. Blackhouse's idea."

Edge finished his beer and looked ruefully into the foam clinging to the sides of the glass. "I'll take the room and bath," he said, and pushed the forty cents towards Alton. "Wouldn't want to offend Mrs. Blackhouse with the dirt under my nails."

"I'm unimportant, young man!"

The voice came from the doorway. Alton nodded a greeting as the half-breed turned. The woman was fat, fifty and may once have been pretty, even beautiful. But time had carved the lines of bitterness into the set of her flabby features. She wore a shapeless black dress and her grey hair was held in a severe bun on the crown of her head. Even in the shade of the covered sidewalk, she continued to hold a white parasol aloft. She stood firmly just beyond the threshold of the saloon doorway, in an attitude which suggested nothing on earth would lure her through the batswings.

"Afternoon, ma'am," Alton said deferentially.

Mrs. Blackhouse ignored him, fixing Edge with an unblinking, malevolent stare. "It is the moral tone of Seascape which concerns me. We are proud of our town and despise violence even more than the loose ways of the so-called entertainers who have invaded us."

"Seems to me the advance was in the opposite direction, lady," Edge said.

"Many were tempted," she allowed. "By frustrated avarice and an even more basic urge. But I fear your act of viciousness will leave a more lasting impression on them than the sight of great wealth and half-clothed females."

"You hurt the guy they took up to Doc Elkin's?" the bartender exclaimed.

The doorway with a sign over it was to one side of the saloon, adjacent to the end of the bar counter.

18

The sign read: ROOMS THIS WAY. Edge started towards it. "It was him or me, and he had his chance," he called. Then he altered course, turning towards the batswings.

The fat woman barred the exit. "I intend to report the incident to the sheriff when he returns from Portland, young man," she said with menace.

Edge halted on the inner threshold and ran his icy gaze insolently over the bulky figure of the woman. "You'll do what you have to, lady," he said softly. "And I can see you've got plenty of body to be busy with."

Mrs. Blackhouse had a pasty complexion. Abruptly, the flabby flesh of her cheeks flushed. "Well I never!" she gasped, insulted.

"Guess that doesn't worry Mr. Blackhouse no more," Edge said, and went forward.

The woman held her position for a moment, then sidestepped hurriedly out of the half-breed's path. "My husband has been dead these past fifteen years!" she hurled at him as he stepped down from the sidewalk.

"My condolences," Edge said, sliding the Winchester from the saddleboot. "To your husband for being married to somebody like you."

The woman's color deepened. She tried to hurl a retort, but managed to vent only an inarticulate croak. Then she whirled with a swish of dress fabric and waddled along the sidewalk. Edge looked beyond her, to the carny midway at the end of the street. The showmen who had helped carry Turk to the town doctor were now back at their tents and doing some business. The big gold exhibit still had the largest crowd and some of the customers who emerged from the rear of the tent returned to join the end of the line for a second look. Others moved along the midway,

19

prepared to be encouraged into spending a little money elsewhere. Mrs. Blackhouse stood in front of the Seascape Bank for a few moments, ramrod stiff, watching her fellow citizens disregarding her advice. Then she pivoted and waddled through the bank doorway.

Edge looked across the deserted street, towards a two story building with a sign proclaiming it was the office of the Seascape Lumber Company. "What day is it, feller?" he called into the saloon.

Alton was wiping and polishing the beer glass the half-breed had used. "Sunday."

It meant the blinds at the windows and doors of the company office were not simply drawn against the sun. As he swung to re-enter the saloon, carrying the Winchester, his attention was once more captured by the carny midway. A buggy drawn by a high-stepping white horse was heading sedately towards town from the east. Holding the reins was an incredibly fat man who smiled brightly at the men and touched his hat to the women who greeted him. As the buggy came clear of the midway and on to the street, the half-breed saw its driver was even fatter than he had seemed on first impression.

He must have weighed at least three hundred and fifty pounds, all of it stacked on to a five and a half feet frame. His girth was enormous, his belly seeming to begin beneath the lowest of his many chins and sagging over his belt to rest on his thick thighs. His face was round, with bright, sunken eyes, bulging cheeks and a protruding mouth. He was sweating a great deal, the moisture oozing across the scarlet flesh of his face faster than he could mop it away with a handerchief. His tight-fitting shirt, which clung to every flabby bulge of his torso had been changed from white to grey by sweat. Even his dark colored pants, encasing him like a second skin, looked like they might drip water if they were wrung out. But he was happy in his discomfort, still showing twin rows of even, white teeth as he reined the black gelding to a halt outside the saloon. It was difficult to guess accurately at his age, which could have been anything from thirty to fifty. For in having to stretch over the obese flesh, the skin remained unwrinkled.

"Good day to you!" he greeted brightly as he eased off the buggy seat and swung himself carefully to the ground. The wheel springs gave a groan of relief and the buggy's body was raised at least three inches higher when free of the man's weight. "Am I going to have some company in this hostelry?"

He wore spurs, which jingled in cheerful accompaniment to his mood as the fat man patted the gelding's neck and hitched the reins to the rail. He also wore a matched pair of gold-plated, ivory-butted Beaumont-Adams revolvers in tooled-leather holsters tied down at his thighs. His index fingers looked too thick to fit between triggers and guards.

"Doubt they've got a bathtub big enough for the both of us," Edge said, and re-entered the saloon.

Every swell of fat trembled when the man laughed.

"Haven't got one big enough for me on my own," he answered, hauling himself up on to the sidewalk to trail the half-breed. "Reason I have to ride out down the coast to find a quiet stretch of ocean. Trouble is, I'm sweating like a pig again time I've made the haul back to town. Two cold beers, Herb. For me and my fellow guest."

Edge had almost reached the doorway which led to the rooms for rent.

"The stranger don't allow folks to buy him drinks, Mr. French," the bartender answered, beginning to draw a beer.

The fat man hauled a chair away from a table and

21

dropped into it gratefully. He used the handkerchief to wipe more sweat from his face, then took off his hat to fan himself. He was bald except for a crescent of sandy hair above each ear. "So I'll drink alone," he said with a shrug that caused the chair to creak. "Make my tab a little lighter." He shook with laughter again. "Won't do the same for me, though."

Edge went through the doorway into a hall that made a right angle turn to run through the rear of the saloon.

"Any room with an open door!" Alton called after him. "Tub and pitcher down at the end. You have to fill 'em yourself. Pump marked salt water."

There was only one of the six doors closed. Edge chose the room at the far end because it was closest to a doorway which gave on to the yard behind the saloon. The two pumps were immediately outside and he only had to tote the pitchers of water a short way. The room was spartanly-furnished, but clean. The bed-linen was sparklingly white: very appealing to Edge who had been sleeping under the stars for more nights than he could remember. But he stuck to the rules of the room rental.

He drew the drape curtain across the recently cleaned window and set the tub down alongside the bed. Then he made a dozen round trips to the salt water pump to fill it almost to the brim. There was kindling beneath a fire-blackened pot in the yard, but the icy cold ocean water felt too good to spoil with heat. There was no key in the door lock and no bolts, so when he had stripped almost naked, he lowered himself into the chill water so that he faced the closed door. This put his back to the window but sometimes a man could not cover all the angles as well as he would like. He had to be content with the best he was able to do. So, with at least one man in town who had

22

good reason to hate him, the half-breed had placed the Winchester on the bed and the Colt on the floor immediately beside the tub: both within a two-feet, easy reach.

The item of apparel which he continued to wear as he sat in the tub, enjoying the shock of coldness against his tacky skin, looked at first glance like mere ornamentation. It was a string of dully-colored beads, threaded on to a leather thong which was looped around his neck. In fact, it served a useful purpose for, attached to it at the rear, beneath the fringe of long black hair, was a buck-skin pouch. In this pouch nestled a sharply honed open cut-throat razor. This razor, like the scar tissue which marred the even coffee color of his hard skin at the left shoulder, right hip and left thigh, was a relic of the war Between the States. The reason for carrying it so, and the speed and expertise with which he used it for purposes other than shaving, could also be traced back to this traumatic opening sequence that had pitched him into a life of violence.

But now he did use the razor to scrape the tough bristles from his lean face—after cleaning the dirt from his body with a fragment of soap a former guest had left in the tub. Then, still abiding by Alton's rules, he wedged a pillow between the back of his head and the wall. And he slept. It was the usual dreamless sleep of a man with a clear conscience. But, again, normal for the lean, hard-bodied half-breed, a shallow sleep. Giving him rest without drifting him too deeply into the slough of unawareness. Body and mind were relaxed, but constantly on the verge of waking to instant total recall of the immediate past and familiarity with his surroundings. Had he rode into Seascape amid peace and tranquility and received a friendly greeting from all, he would have slept in the same manner. For it was the natural way with a man who had been brushed so often by death: and who had made so many enemies in order to survive.

So it was that he came awake when a floorboard creaked immediately outside the room door. He knew where he was and what had happened. The only change in the room since he went to sleep was in the level of light filtering through the drape curtains. It was no so bright and was tinting from yellow to red as the afternoon sun heralded the evening by sinking towards the horizon of the ocean. He made a conscious decision to choose the Winchester and pumped the action to feed a shell into the breech as he swung the rifle from the bed. Knuckles rapped on the door and he rested the rifle barrel across the vee of his naked knees.

"Not locked," he called.

The door swung open and Herb Alton gulped as he looked at the rifle pointed towards him. "Hey, I might have been a woman," he said shakily.

"In which case I might have been happier to see you," the half-breed answered. With the door open, he could hear a murmuring of talk from the saloon, accompanied by the clink of glasses against a background of plaintive mouth-organ music. He eased the winchester's hammer back to the rest and tossed the rifle on to the bed.

Alton breathed more easily. "I just come to say there's a guy'd like to see you. Some one from the carny. And also, I reckon you've had more than your forty centsworth."

"You said the room was mine for as long as it took for me to have the bath," Edge reminded the bartender, and eased himself upright. "I had a lot of trail dirt to scrub off."

There was nothing vulnerable about the tall, lean

man. Even naked and toweling the running water from his body, he looked dangerously ready to unleash lightning violence. And now that his face was cleaned of dirt and stubble the degree of impassive coldness in his blue eyes was even more menacing. He remained close to the bed with the rifle lying obscenely across the patchwork quilt.

"That's okay," the bartender allowed, trying to make it sound like a favor. "The guy that wants to see you is the dude with the gold he charges folks to look at."

Edge nodded. "Tell him I'll be right out." He grinned. "And close the door. The fat dame might walk past and get you closed down for having a naked man in one of your rooms."

"Mrs. Blackhouse never comes into my saloon," Alton answered. "She doesn't approve of strong drink."

"We've all got our prejudices," the half-breed said. "Me, I've got this thing about not being watched when I'm naked. By a man, anyway, and we've already established what you are."

"I'm goin'," Alton stammered, and closed the door hurriedly.

Edge wasted no time in dressing, but not in consideration for the man who was waiting to see him. While the door had been open, cold air had wafted into the room, fresh with a salty tang which told it was being breezed on to shore from the ocean. Its coolness completed the process of refreshment the half-breed had derived from the bath and the sleep. But in contrast to earlier, the feel of the sweat-stiffened clothing against his body was welcome.

If not a new man, he at least felt a less weary one as he let himself out of the room, closing the door on

25

the tub of dirt-scummed water. He almost became a dead one.

He heard the hiss of the knife through the murky air of the hallway before he sensed another presence. It came at him from outside, spinning in through the open doorway to the yard. His head swung around just enough for his narrowed eyes to catch a glimpse of Jo Jo Lamont. She was still showing a lot of cleavage between the powdered swells of her upthrust breasts. But her legs were concealed now, beneath the long, full skirt of her low-cut green dress. She was standing square on to the open doorway, leaning forward slightly and with her right arm still stretched out in front of her after releasing the knife.

Edge dropped to his knees and powered to the side, falling away from girl and the spinning knife. He had been carrying the Winchester low on his left and it was trapped under his hip as he hit the floor. But the Colt was clear of the holster before the knife bit deep into the door jamb.

"Freeze, or burn in hell!" he rasped.

Jo Jo was still leaning forward, but had started to swing her body around for a lunge away from the doorway. An undoubted willingness to back up the threat with the deed was blatant in the half-breed's voice. The girl became like a stone statue, held on the very brink of toppling from the canting, twisted posture.

A door rattled open at the far end of the hallway. Floorboards creaked under the great weight. "My, what's this?" The easy, ready-to-laugh tone confirmed that the obese French had emerged from his room.

"None of your business," Edge muttered, continuing to keep his eyes and the revolver on the girl as he eased up on to his haunches and then stood erect. A fast glance at the hilt of the knife showed it was a match for the one Turk had hurled at him. Its position in the door jamb showed it would have buried its point between his shoulder blades had he not powered down out of its path.

"Enough said," the fat responded and there was a hollow ring to his laughter. "Far be it from Clarence French to intervene when a man has been bowled off his feet by a young lady."

The floorboards began to creak rhythmically as the fat man headed for the right angle turn which led to the saloon. The girl had straightened, but her feet remained firmly planted on the ground. Now that the heat and brightness had gone out of the day, the evening light flattered her shallow prettiness.

"You and Turk take it in turns tossing knives at each other?" Edge asked, the harshness extracted from his tone.

"We've spent a lot of time together," she responded sullenly. "He taught me how to use the knives. The kind of jerkwater, no-business towns we get to, I've had plenty of practice."

"You always pick targets without asking permission first?" He beckoned with the rifle for her to come in through the doorway.

"You can put away the gun," she said, dragging her feet as she entered the hallway. "I only brought one knife. I knew I wouldn't get a second chance if I missed first time."

"Pretty smart for someone as dumb as you," Edge told her, launching a back heel kick at the door. It burst open and banged back against the inner wall.

"The sawbones says Turk'll never be able to throw a knife with his right hand again," Jo Jo accused, fear overlaying her sullenness now, as Edge jerked the Winchester to signal her into the room. "Maybe never

27

be able to pick one up if the nerves are cut like he thinks."

"So you figured to make me bleed for him?" Edge asked as Jo Jo swung in front of him to enter the room. She did a pathetic little run, to get beyond his reach fast.

Trapped inside the room, she swung around and flared with anger. "For me, you vicious sonofabitch!" she snarled. "We were heading for San Francisco. One of the theatres down there was going to give Turk and me a long-term contract. We could have really made the big time."

Her eyes glowed brighter. Not entirely with anger now. In anticipation of the dream that might have been. Edge had seen there was nowhere on the outside of the dress where she could carry a second knife. He holstered the Colt and jerked the blade out of the doorjamb. Jo Jo caught her breath.

"What are you gonna do?" she gasped as he advanced into the room.

He left the door open. Somebody was still playing the mouth organ but the buzz of conversation had trailed away. It was the same tune, sounding sadder than ever as the only disturbance against the silence.

"Kill you, maybe," he said.

She jerked a hand to her vividly painted lips, muffling the squeal of terror. Then she took a step backwards. Another cry was vented as she banged against the foot of the bed and tumbled down on to it. "Please!" she begged as Edge halted, towering over her. "It was crazy. I know it. But I just sat out at the camp getting madder and madder about what you done to Turk. Some of them said I oughta do something about it. They gave me some rye. I just . . ."

He could smell the liquor on her breath. It was stronger than the scent of fear-pumped sweat that

28

rose from her cheaply perfumed flesh. Her big breasts rose and fell rapidly. Her features were contorted, manifesting her thought processes as her mind sought frantically for a way out. Her eyes were fastened upon the knife held loosely in Edge's right hand. Then the idea hit her. She tore her gaze away and fixed it on his face. In the fading light her expression was an ugly parody of panting passion.

"I'll do anything!" she offered breathlessly. "Anything you want, only please don't cut me."

"Close your eyes," the half-breed ordered softly.

Jo Jo did so, snapping down the blackened lids and screwing them tight. Her hands lay at her sides and she bunched them into frightened fists. Edge threw the knife underarm. It made a solid thud as the point sank into the wooden bedhead. The girl shuddered, then held her breath. But she kept her eyes screwed shut. Her body was ramrod stiff.

"There's something you should know," she whispered as Edge stooped down at the side of the bed, leaning the Winchester against the wall.

"My Pa told me everything about what you have in mind," he said.

Despite everything, Jo Jo could still blush. "I'm a virgin," she rasped her color deepening, and spreading to suffuse her flesh from the line of the blonde hair at the top of her forehead to creep to the full extent of the rises of her breasts where the neckline of the dress cradled them.

"That'll be nice for somebody," Edge said as he straightened up again. The filled tub of water was heavy, but he lifted it with ease. Then he thrust it out in front of him, held it for a moment above the taut-bodied, prostrate girl: and tipped it.

The scummy, filthy water cascaded over her from head to waist, sending her hair into disarray and past-ing the dress fabric to her body. She shrieked and sprang into a sitting position, fisting the water from her eyes as Edge let the bathtub clatter to the floor. Heavy, running footfalls sounded in the hallway. The music had stopped.

"You beast!" Jo Jo screamed at him as he picked up the Winchester from where it leaned against the wall. She tore her gaze away from him to stare down at the sodden gown. The water had done something to the stiffening which held the bodice to the curves of her breasts. She managed to clutch the fabric to her just before it folded away to expose her. "This is the only decent dress I've got!" she sobbed. "You've ruined it."

"I've only got one life," he hissed. "You and your partner weren't trying to improve it by carving holes in my back. Either of you give me so much as a sharp glance from now on, you're dead."

"Hey, what's goin' on?" Alton yelled, at the forefront of the group crowded into the doorway.

Jo Jo became aware of the watching men. Behind Alton, she recognized the dark-skinned tiger trainer, the dude-dressed Case, three of the spielers from the other sideshows and one of the guards from the big gold exhibit.

"I don't allow men to have girls in my rooms!" Alton accused harshly.

Edge canted the Winchester across his shoulder and curled back his lips to show a cold grin. "She wasn't had, feller," he said. "She figured to get me to do a little breaking and entering—but I poured cold water on the idea."

The girl vented another shriek and, still holding the sagging fabric against her breasts, she lunged up from the bed and raced towards the doorway. The group of men parted to give her an exit and she curved between them without slackening her pace. She made for the rear door from the hallway.

"Like you saw," the half-breed muttered. "She gives every impression of still being chaste."

31

CHAPTER THREE

"Have a drink, Mr.—"

"Edge," the half-breed supplied as he dropped into a chair across the table from Case. "Speak your piece."

The dude shrugged acceptance of Edge's manner and filled a shot glass from a three-quarters full bottle of whiskey. Both the glass and whiskey bottle had been on the table when Case led the half-breed to it. Case had been about to signal Alton to fetch another glass, but now he let his arm fall.

The dark-skinned animal trainer began to play his mouth organ again. The three spielers and the guard re-started a game of five-card stud. The obese Clarence French, still sweating despite the cool evening air flowing in over and under the closed batswings, was beating time to the music with two fingers of each hand on the table top. He had been the only patron of the saloon not to investigate the disturbance down the hallway.

32

"You're looking for work, I hear?" Case asked.

"Don't believe everything you hear, feller," the half-breed answered. "But sometimes the rumors are right."

"I can offer you a job."

"To kill somebody?"

Case was not taken aback by the response. "Not specifically, no. Although it could possibly prove necessary—in undertaking the work."

"Pay?"

"A hundred dollars a week."

Edge did not hesitate. He nodded. "Chance of a five dollar advance?"

Case smiled. He had a very pleasant face when he smiled. The expression added animation without color. Edge had noticed that out on the midway when Case was collecting money at the entrance to his exhibit. "You need it for something special, Edge?" His billfold was slender, but most of the bills inside were fifties and hundreds. He found a five spot and passed it across the table.

"Appreciate it," the half-breed said, and raised his voice. "Alton, fetch me a beer."

The two men regarded each other in an easy silence while the bartender drew the drink and fetched it to the table. Case didn't smile anymore, but he seemed pleased with what he saw—satisfied that, close up, the impression he had received of Edge in the afternoon was an accurate one. The half-breed saw that Case was older than he had seemed at first glance. Perhaps forty-five. And not so soft. His build was small and he had the pallor of a man unused to the outdoor life. His hands, spotlessly clean and well manicured, had never done a day's hard work of the manual kind. But there was a certain inbred toughness about the set of his regular features. The mouthline suggested it gave

33

orders with authority and the dark eyes seemed capable of offering a solid challenge to anybody who disobeyed the orders. And there was a wiry strength in his build which promised a physical back-up.

Alton accepted the five dollar bill with a smile after he had set down the beer. "Rooms are two dollars a night if you're interested."

"Edge will be staying out at the camp if he agrees to work for me, Alton," Case said.

"I've taken your money," Edge said flatly after taking a swallow at the beer. "So I'm working for you."

"Without knowing what the job is?" Case was still not surprised.

"I know what it's not."

The bartender shook his head, giving up for all time efforts to understand the tall stranger. Then he went to get the change, taking a roundbout course so that he could light the saloon's lamps against the advancing night. As if the kerosene glow acted as a beacon for the thirsty and the lonely, new patrons began to push in through the batswings. They were a mixture of local citizens and people from the carny.

"Alton didn't put up his drink prices," Edge said to fill the time while the bartender made change for the five.

Case smiled and the half-breed got the impression that the dude always felt happiest when money was the topic of conversation. "He'll have to live in the town after we've left. But he likes to make a few dollars. So he bows to the wishes of the Blackhouse woman on the one hand and takes our money with the other." Then he grimaced. "I haven't been in this business long, Edge. But I've run up against more than enough people like Mrs. Blackhouse. The kind that think beds are only for kneeling down and praying beside and a good time is walking home from church on Sunday. Why, we were in a town in Wyoming where they had a sheriff named Shorty Dodge . . ."

Alton returned to the table and dropped the four ninety-five hurriedly into Edge's outstretched hand. Then he scuttled back to attend to the sudden influx of custom. Case changed the subject immediately.

"I'm offering you a hundred a week to guard my gold until the end of the week."

"Short job."

"But the pay's good."

Edge sipped his beer. "Can't argue with that. Guess Grainger and his buddies didn't do any complaining, either."

Case grimaced. "Those men are on two dollars a day."

A couple of the local citizens, who seemed to have had more than enough liquor before coming to the saloon, were urging the harmonica player to get something more cheerful out of his instrument.

"Keep talking, feller," Edge invited.

"The job will involve watching the guards as much as taking care of the big gold," Case responded, licking his lips. His normal level of speech was not high, but now it became a whisper as he shot a glance at the men playing poker. "I don't trust Grainger and the others. I haven't seen or heard anything I can pin down, but there's something about their attitude. You saw them this afternoon. You can see Dana Breeze over there playing poker now. What do you think of them?"

Edge sipped his beer. "They're tough, they're mean and they look like they can use the guns they carry. I never judge people by appearances. But for a hundred dollars I'm happy you have doubts."

35

"I'm a businessman, Edge," Case said as the animal trainer submitted to the urgings and altered his style of music. "I've learned that appearances can sometimes be deceptive. But after a little study and a few facts, a man can be judged. Take yourself for instance. You can handle yourself and you can be tougher and meaner and more vicious than all four of my guards put together when the occasion demands —if you'll excuse me for saying so?"

"You'll know when you get out of line," the half-breed allowed wryly.

"But you're broke and won't even accept a free drink. To my mind, that makes you a man of principle. An honest man."

Edge curled back his lips to show a sardonic smile. "I knew I had to have at least one redeeming feature, feller. What's yours? Being rich don't count. And being stupid sure don't, either."

Case looked as if he might flare into anger at the insult. Edge ignored him for a few moments, to watch an argument at another table. The young fire-eater was trying to dissuade the exotic dancer from getting up to give a free show. The girl was about eighteen, a good-looking redhead with a slender figure. She was the only female in the saloon and getting a lot of attention. The two local drunks and the fat Clarence French were the loudest in urging her to ignore her escort's pleas. She looked a little drunk herself. Or perhaps it was just that she had dancing in her blood and the music was getting to her.

"Meaning what, Edge?" Case asked tautly.

"Meaning that it's stupid to haul a million dollars-worth of gold all over this kind of country," the half-breed answered, still watching the girl as she tore free of the young man's grasp. "And because of the job

I've just taken, I've got to believe your show isn't a fake."

A loud cheer greeted the girl's freedom. Of the watchers, only the young man and the bartender were less than happy as the girl glided smoothly into an open area between the tables. Alton looked anxious. The young man was angry.

"It's no fake!" Case rasped, soft but emphatic. "Why I'm doing it is my business. Did I ask you questions?"

The girl had a dark skin, perhaps from the sun or maybe from heritage. Even darker eyes, which flashed with unadulterated enjoyment as she began to sway her body and move her limbs in time with the music.

Edge shrugged. "Forget I asked, feller."

Case smiled. "Good. We understand each other. I ask you only to protect my gold and will not question the methods you adopt to achieve it."

"First time you do, I'll take what I'm owed. And you can find somebody else to guard you against the dangers of your own stupidity."

Once more, Case's anger rose close to breaking surface. But he held it in check. The half-breed had made up his mind and he was obviously not the kind of man to be swayed by words. He was just the kind of man for the job he had accepted. Even sitting, relaxed in the chair, sipping the beer and watching the sinewy, erotic motions of the girl's body, the tall half-breed exuded a sense of latent evil and power, ever-ready to be unleashed at the slightest provocation.

"There's going to be trouble," Case said softly.

"I reckon," Edge agreed.

Despite his non-demonstrative enjoyment of the girl's sensuous dancing, he was not giving her his undivided attention. He was aware of the conflicting emotions which seemed to have a physical presence in the saloon's atmosphere, heavy with the smells of cigar smoke, spilled liquor and burning kerosene.

"The young man is Walter Peat," Case supplied. "The girl's Arabella. Nobody knows her surname. He'd marry her tomorrow if she'd have him."

"This carny's full of crazy people," Edge muttered and turned up the corners of his mouth in a quiet grin as he shot a sidelong glance at Case, and saw the dude was again having to struggle to hold back his anger. The half-breed didn't like working for another man. When it was necessary, he made sure that the money bought only his labor: that all else stayed equal.

Arabella was having fun. She had a good body and was a good dancer. She knew it and enjoyed combining the two natural talents for the entertainment of men. And the more the all-male audience reacted, wearing their lust on deeply-colored, sweating faces, the greater became her delight in her own ability to arouse such passions. And the higher Walter Peat's anger became.

"You ready to start work?" Case asked.

Edge finished his beer. "Sure thing."

Both men rose from the table. Arabella became a little more adventurous as the tempo of the music was stepped up. She stooped, clutched the hem of her long skirt and began to draw it upwards, unveiling her bare legs a senuous inch at a time. She continued to writhe her body, wearing a triumphant smile as her audience clapped, stamped their feet and whistled and roared in ecstatic approval. Then, when one of the laughing drunks lunged off his chair and staggered towards her, she emitted a high-pitched peal of her own laughter and she skipped lightly away from him. She had the skirt up around her waist now, the dark-skinned slenderness of her long legs completely revealed from ankles to thighs.

The drunk pulled up short and then began a reeling turn, his lust-bright eyes blinking in the lamp light as he tried to spot the girl. He saw her, made another lunge and missed again. The enjoyment of the audience increased and their laughter rose. He heard the high-pitched trill of Arabella above all the other noise. He whirled, failed to see the girl, but raked his eyes over the gleeful faces of the audience. Rightly or wrongly, he became convinced that the men were laughing in scorn at his attempts to capture the wanton dancer.

"Quit it, Rube!" the bartender yelled above the new explosion of sound. "Everybody quieten down or I'll close up the place."

But nobody took any notice of the threat. Edge and Case headed for the batswings. The harmonica player continued to blare his music. Arabella responded to the sound with even wilder abandon. The audience roared. Rube's expression became mean. His sense of being viewed with contempt had the effect of sobering him. He timed his move better now, and when he reached for the swirling, high-kicking girl, he made contact. His arms snaked around her from behind, his hands splaying and then closed to fasten over the small mounds of her breasts.

The dark-skinned man playing the mouth organ had his eyes closed, his mind lost in the frenetic world of his own music. Abruptly, Arabella vented a piercing scream. Whether from the pain of Rube's grip or terror that she had lost her power over the men, it was difficult to tell. Then, even before the keening sound had faded, the music stopped. Was curtailed without warning, as Peat launched himself from his chair, one arm lashing out. His fist crashed into the side of the

39

musician's head. The man was toppled sideways off his chair. He smacked hard to the floor with a cry of mixed pain and alarm as his harmonica slipped from his fingers to scale across the room.

"Wait!" Arabella yelled, grimacing as the kneading fingers of the now grinning Rube probed into her flesh and he hugged her body to his.

But Peat had expended his rage in the single blow. His voice was cold and his expression was impassive as he spoke into the sudden silence that had descended upon the saloon in the wake of the scream. "You been hanging out the sign long enough, Ara!" he told her. "Now's the time you gotta deliver."

Then he swung away and strode to where Edge and Case had halted at the batswings.

"*Yippppeee!*" Rube exclaimed, and thudded a knee into the small of the girl's back.

She groaned and arched her body. Rube stepped backwards and hauled at the girl, dragging her down to the floor.

"Stop it!" Alton shrieked. "Somebody do something."

Clarence French sipped his beer and smiled. The rest of the audience were about evenly divided in approving or disapproving of the drunk's actions as he sought to hold the struggling girl. The men from the carny were among those who watched with eager anticipation.

"Go to it, feller!" Dana Breeze snarled. "Her boyfriend's right. She's been wavin' it in front of the guys ever since we hit the trail with the carny. About time she did more than flash it."

Peat had halted and was having second thoughts about his decision to abandon the girl to her fate.

"Women and gold," Edge said softly. "Both can send a guy crazy."

40

Anguish replaced the cold blackness in Peat's eyes and he pivoted. "Let her alone!" he screamed.

Rube had a hand on Arabella's skirt and was hauling on the fabric to expose her legs again. Fear had paralyzed the girl into rigid submission. The shouts of encouragement faded and all eyes swung towards the young man, whose high anger was causing him to shudder. He took a step forward, knocking over a chair. Breeze hadn't only been playing poker. As he whirled to face the youngster, he almost overbalanced. He fumbled in drawing the sixgun from the tied-down holster. But it was clear, cocked and aimed at Peat before the young man could take another step. Gasps rippled from several throats. The animal trainer rose on to all fours and scuttled out of the firing line.

"Oh, dear, dear me!" he muttered in a strange sing-song English accent. He snatched up his mouth organ as if it was the most precious thing he possessed.

Breeze's body swayed, but the Remington stayed firmly aimed at Peat. "You said it right the first time, Walt," he rasped.

"Breeze!" Case barked. "Holster that gun!"

A sneer spread across the hard-eyed face of the guard. "Don't you give me orders on my night off, Mr. goddamn Roger goddamn rich Case," he snarled. "The dame's been askin' for it, and she's gonna get it. From every man who can raise what it takes."

As he swung to address the dude, the Remington swung with him. Both his gaze and the gun muzzle traveled in too great an arc, brushing over Edge. Breeze made his sneer heavier with contempt. "You, too, mister!" he slurred. "I'd really get a belt out of blasting you for sticking your oar in where it's not wanted."

"I really think this thing has gone far enough,"

41

Clarence French announced pompously, for once not looking happy.

"Don't figure to stick anything in anywhere," the half-breed replied softly, tightening his left-handed grip around the Winchester.

"I sure as hell do!" Rube yelled, his hands fumbling at Arabella's underwear.

"Walter!" the girl shrieked.

"Oh, dear, dear me!" the animal trainer muttered, gulping.

"That's real fine," Breeze said, tearing his wild stare away from Edge's cool gaze. The Remington swung away, too. "Hold it, Walt!" he demanded, covering the youngster just as Peat was about to respond once more to Arabella's plea.

"Please, stop it, somebody!" the bartender implored, his eyes wide behind the spectacle lenses.

Edge's left arm swung, thudding the stock of the rifle against his shoulder. His right hand flashed up, pumped the action, and his index finger caressed the trigger.

"Breeze!" Clarence French exclaimed.

But the hard-eyed guard had only time to turn his head. He was still square-on to Walter Peat, the Remington aimed at the youngster, when the rifle exploded the loudest sound yet in the saloon.

"Oh, dear, dear me!" the animal trainer shrieked, and went flat to the floor again.

Others joined him, while French was among those who leaped upright in reaction to the shot. Alton screamed and plunged into a crouch behind the protection of his bar counter. Dana Breeze had no time to scream or start any voluntary movement. The .44 calibre bullet rifled into one of the guard's hard eyes. The angle of entry was acute. The lead bored behind the bridge of the man's nose, gouged through the

42

rear of the other eyeball and burst clear at the far side of his head. Blood gushed from the exploded eye, cascaded down his nose and sprayed from the exit wound. His other eye became scarlet as he crashed backwards over a table. The Remington slipped from his nerveless fingers and the table collapsed beneath him. Coins and playing cards, a bottle and four glasses scattered across the floor. The bullet broke a bottle on a shelf behind the bar and imbedded itself in the woodwork. For stretched seconds, as the pool of blood around the dead man's head grew wider, the distant crashing of ocean breakers was the only sound to disturb the taut stillness of the saloon.

Then there was a fast series of metallic noises as Edge worked the action of the Winchester. The expended shell was ejected and a fresh one thudded into the breech. "Warned him this afternoon," the half-breed said coldly. "Not to point a gun at me. Only tell anyone anything the once."

Rube was petrified by the explosion of violence. Was probably unaware of what was happening as Arabella tore free of his abruptly weak hands and scrambled upright, adjusting her clothing. Clarence French looked angry. The bartender rose into sight, a sick expression on his face. Case gave a low whistle. Almost everybody was looking at Edge as the half-breed lowered the rifle and eased the hammer to the rest.

But not the girl. She vented a dry sob and lunged towards Peat. Not the youngster, either. He side-stepped to evade her outstretched arms, then plunged past her.

"Wait!"

Her cry drew everyone's attention to a new center of interest. Rube was the last to react, and by that time Walter Peat had lurched to a halt in front of him. Rube was still kneeling on the floor. Peat stooped, dragging a hand out of his shirt pocket. The hand went to his mouth and he bent lower. His other hand dragged along the floor and a match flared.

"No, Walt!" the girl implored.

"Oh, goodness gracious me!" the animal trainer exclaimed, and covered his face with his hands.

Rube's need was greater, but he had neither the time nor the strength to protect himself. Walt hissed out his breath and flicked the match in front of his mouth. A great, searing streak of orange and blue flame speared out from his lips. Rube screamed and fell backwards. His hair was ablaze and smoke puffed from his eyebrows. He got his hands to his face now, to claw at the agonizing flesh as he twitched and rolled on the floor. Peat went down on to his haunches and tossed more chemical at his mouth. He struck a second match and breathed another stream of fire, searing it across the backs of the screaming Rube's hands.

Then Arabella reached her partner, grasped his shoulders and yanked him away. The sounds of agony from Rube reached a crescendo as he rolled and writhed, alternately beating at his flaming hair and clawing at his blistered flesh. Spilled whiskey added fuel to the flames, until French lunged forward. The fat man hurled beer over the flaring head. Other men were ejected from their shocked immobility and took the cue. The flames surrendered to the cascade of beer and hissed out.

The animal trainer sprang to his feet and sprinted for the doors. "Pardon me, sahibs!" he called, bobbing his head deferentially to Edge and Case as he approached them. "This no place for honorable highborn Nepalese boy."

"You fellers are getting everywhere," the half-breed muttered as he stepped aside to let the man reach the batswings.

Mrs. Blackhouse, hurriedly dressed and with night-cream pasted to her cheeks, gave a cry of alarm as the flung open doors almost knocked her off her feet. "I knew it, I knew it!" she shrieked. "I told you! Let this riff-raff into town and there'd be trouble!"

She didn't venture inside, but stood on the side-walk, her hands curled over the top of the batswings, holding the doors firmly closed. Edge canted the Winchester across his shoulder as he turned towards the exit.

"Like to leave, lady," he said softly.

"You!" the guardian of Seascape's morals accused, recognizing the half-breed after her shocked eyes had taken in the sight of the dead man and the terribly injured one. "I should have known you'd be involved!"

"Get Doc Elkins, ma'am!" somebody pleaded. "Rube Whitaker's hurt pretty bad."

"Better do like the man says," Edge urged, moving towards the batswings, with Case hard on his heels. "Unless you want the feller to suffer. On account of he was the hothead that started the trouble."

The woman backed away from the doorway, releasing her grip. "Which you doubtless had a large part in!" she said with heavy contempt.

Edge pushed out through the batswings and saw a large crowd had gathered on the street, drawn by the shot and the screams. "Me?" he said, showed his teeth in a narrow-eyed, cold grin, then pursed his lips and spat into the dust beyond the sidewalk. "I was just in the saloon shooting the Breeze."

CHAPTER FOUR

Nobody had taken care of Edge's horse. The stallion was still hitched to the rail outside the saloon, but he looked content and rested. Unworried by the explosion of violence that had recently erupted. The half-breed did not normally keep a horse for long. This stallion had been his mount for longer than usual and was familiar with sudden bursts of gunfire and the venting of agonies which often ensued.

"We're camped south of town," Case explained, and for the first time he revealed that the events in the saloon had got to him. There was a tremor in his voice. And he set a fast pace along the street, as if anxious to retreat from the curious stares of the crowd.

Edge, with the rifle still resting across his shoulder, stayed on the ground and led the horse in the wake of Case. It wasn't far to the camp. As they turned into a side street between the church and the law office, Edge noted that all sign of the carny had been

46

eradicated from where the trail ran into the end of town.

"Moving out tomorrow?" he asked.

The side street was a short one, lined by frame houses. Where it ended, a logging trail cut into the timber. Firelight flickered from somewhere deep in the woods.

"A few hours is all a town the size of this is worth," Case replied, his nerves under control again. "If we had reached here this morning we'd have been gone by noon. But some damn Rogue River Indians spooked the horses at dawn. Took us three hours to round them up after they scattered."

"Some good Indians," Edge said lightly. "Hadn't have been for them I'd most likely be felling red-woods tomorrow. For a lot less than you're paying me."

"And this is more your line of work," Case suggested.

The half-breed spat into the brush at the side of the trail. "You said it awhile back, feller. We understand each other."

They finished the walk to the campsite in silence. There were eleven wagons, all of them covered. Ten of them were painted with signs on the side canvases and rear flaps, using much the same words as had been on the boards set up in front of the tents flanking the midway. These ten were parked in two ranks, nose-to-tail, in an arc around one side of a clearing in which a number of cooking fires were burning low. The odd one out was parked on the far side of the clearing and further back from the fires than the others. It was a brand new wagon and the still-clean canvas had no lettering or pictures painted on it. What it did have was a guard perched on the seat and another leaning against the tailgate. Both had rifles. Neither was Grainger. They eyed the half-breed

47

closely as Edge veered away from Case, leading the stallion over to the remuda of horses ground hobbled at the back of the clearing. Unsaddling his mount, Edge sensed many other pairs of eyes watching him: from the wagons and from the small groups clustering around the fires. He was conscious that nobody was looking at him with an easy mind. Jo Jo Lamont and Turk—if he had been allowed to return to camp after the doctor was finished with him—were probably the ones pouring the greatest degree of animosity towards him, he guessed. But the atmosphere of hatred hanging over the clearing in the sea-fresh air was more powerful than that which could be generated by just two people.

Grainger confirmed it. "The Nep told us you blasted Dana, Edge!" the burly guard announced harshly.

"Oh, dear, dear me!" the Nepalese singsonged anxiously. "There must be no more trouble. My animals will respond most unfortunately."

As the cinch was unfastened and Edge slid the saddle and bedroll from the stallion, two low, animalistic roars rumbled from one of the wagons.

"I may go now, sahib?" the tiger trainer pleaded. "To quieten my beasts very fast, please?"

"Yeah, get lost, Nep!" Grainger snarled.

Edge had slid the Winchester back into the boot before unsaddling the stallion. Now, as he turned away from the horse, he carried his gear under his left arm. His right hand was close to the butt of the holstered Colt. The stallion began to munch hungrily on the hay spread across the ground.

"We've had enough trouble for one day!" Case snapped.

The Nepalese was hurrying towards one of the wagons which was rocking on its springs as its wild animal cargo moved restlessly in close confinement. Grainger had risen from the side of one of the fires and stepped away, so that his burly frame was silhouetted against the flames. Case, looking smaller than ever by comparison, had stopped just short of the firing line between the two tall men.

"Breeze and me done a lot together, Mr. Case," Grainger said tensely. "Been a lot of places together."

"That fire ain't warm enough for you, be happy to send you where your buddy's gone." As he spoke, Edge released his gear and swung his body half away from Grainger.

The flames crackled and spat. The distant ocean crashed against the foot of the Oregon cliffs. The watchers caught their collective breath. The tigers growled.

"You blasted him when he wasn't lookin'," Grainger accused and there was less power in his voice now. His opening taunt had been impulsive, his mind filled with a desire to avenge the death of his partner. But now he saw the half-breed adopt the stance of an expert gunfighter. And he remembered the coldly calculated act of slicing Turk's arm on the midway.

"He made two mistakes," Edge answered easily as the familiar sound of the harmonica drifted across the clearing. The music was mournful, as it had been in the Seascape Saloon before the tempo was raised to a crescendo which presaged tragedy. The growling of the tigers slackened to a contented purring and the wagon ceased to rock. "He pointed a gun at me after I'd told him it irked me. And he didn't fire it."

Grainger didn't have his Winchester. But he was wearing a gunbelt with a revolver in the holster. He had adopted the sideways-on attitude as a reflex action when Edge turned from unsaddling the stallion. But anger made him tense, and experience warned him he was in the wrong frame of mind to call the ice-cold killer who faced him. He allowed his shoulders to slope and his right hand dropped below the level of the Colt's butt. "I never make mistakes," he growled, and looked at the dude. "I'll need to get a replacement for Breeze."

"I've already got one," Case answered, and jerked a thumb towards Edge.

The Nepalese had stopped the melancholy music and the tigers were quiet and still. The quick intake of breath into a score of throats was audible, as relaxing tension was suddenly drawn taut again.

"Him?"

Edge was picking up his gear, holding it in both hands. But it was obvious he was ready to let it go again.

"I think he's proved himself capable of handling the job," Case said tartly.

Grainger's face showed a scowl in the firelight's flicker. The grunt he vented was just as ugly. "I ain't gonna be happy workin' alongside him."

"Alongside or in front," Edge put in, moving towards the fire closest to the big gold wagon. "Just don't get in back of me."

Grainger responded with another grunt and swung around to squat down beside the fire where he had been previously. The watchers eased into relaxation again and the murmurings of low-voiced conversations became overlayed on the sound of the distant ocean. Edge took a position at the side of the fire so that his back was towards the remuda and he was able to keep Grainger and the two other guards in sight. There was beef stew in the fire-blackened pot hung from a tripod over the glowing embers. He ladled some on to a tin plate taken from his own bedroll. It probably wasn't so good as it tasted, but he hadn't eaten since his dawn breakfast.

Case joined him, careful to sit on a blanket so that his elegantly cut pants and jacket didn't trail in the dirt. He rinsed a dirty mug in a pail of water before pouring coffee. His features were set in lines which suggested he was having to work hard to hold on to his anger again.

"I'm not questioning your methods, Edge," he muttered. "I said I wouldn't. But the job is guard the gold and watch the others. I can't condone you killing them one at a time."

"One at a time or the whole bunch," Edge answered, chewing a tough piece of meat. "Or maybe none of them that's left. Anyway they call it, feller."

"Grainger has got a big mouth. Salter and Wylie can talk up a storm as well. Just try to take it easy, will you?"

The half-breed spat into the fire. "If I take it any easier, I'm liable to go to sleep." As if this really were a possibility, he stood up, sliding the rifle from the saddleboot as he did so. "Like to see what I'm guarding, feller." He grinned. "Providing I don't have to pay no fifty cents now I'm in on the act?"

Case matched the easy humor with his expression and a lightness in his tone as he stood up. "One of the few fringe benefits of your job. Look at it as often as you like for free."

As they approached the rear of the wagon, the guard straightened out of his slouch. His expression altered from subservient to distaste as he looked from Case to Edge.

"Open her up, Wylie," the dude instructed. "You heard what I told Grainger about Edge joining us?"

"I heard," the blond-haired guard growled. "And

51

I'm about as happy as Grainger on account of it. Same goes for Salter, I reckon."

He worked on the pegs holding the tailgate up.

"I don't pay you to be happy," Case chided.

"Just careful," Edge supplemented, and hoisted himself up on to the wagon, drawing aside the flaps.

The others stayed outside, peering in under the flaps. Edge struck a match and surveyed the carny's main attraction. It wasn't much unless the imagination began to work on the sight. Just a cube of bright yellow metal about seven feet along each side, cold to the touch and as smooth as a young girl's skin. It stood in the center of a stout iron grille which added strength to the bed of the wagon.

"How much it weigh?" Edge asked after running a hand over the precious metal and watching the match flame dance in reflection against the gold.

"Three thousand pounds," Case replied. "Give or take an ounce or two."

The match died and Edge spent a few moments working out the sum. "At more than twenty bucks an ounce, who's giving and who's taking?"

Case waited until the half-breed had jumped down from the wagon and Wylie started to refasten the tailgate. He showed a sheepish grin. "In towns like Seascape, who knows what a million dollarsworth of gold looks like? So I only paid a quarter of that for it."

"Glad I didn't have to pay the fifty cents," Edge said. "I'd feel cheated."

"I wouldn't have told you."

The half-breed nodded. "How do you show it?"

"Build the tent over the wagon. Then take off the canvas and supports and let down the tailgate and sides. Used to let them touch it at first, but some of them brought knives and did some scraping. Now we have a barrier all around the wagon to keep it out of reach."

"What about guarding it? On the trail and in camp?"

"I left that to Grainger. He organized it. On the trail I drive and all four guards ride escort. At night they work a rota, two watching while the other pair rest."

"You got any quarrel with that, mister?" Wylie muttered churlishly.

Edge shouldered the Winchester. "Be sure to wake me when you and your partner have finished your stint," he replied, and ambled back to the fire.

Peat and Arabella returned from town as he was spreading his bedroll. They had their arms around each other's waist and the boy was whispering something in the girl's ear to make her giggle. The three spielers were not far behind the couple. Case bedded down on the same side of the fire as Edge, stripping down to his underwear and folding his top clothes carefully before sliding into a sleeping bag. Grainger took a position on the other side of the fire. Like Edge, he removed only his hat and his gunbelt. He took two extra blankets from another bedroll—presumably the one that had belonged to Dana Breeze. The camp became quiet, except for an occasional burst of low laughter from the wagon shared by the fire-eater and the exotic dancer.

"I don't know why Peat wants to marry her," Case said with a sigh, his attempts to get to sleep thwarted by the laughter. "They hate each other one moment and climb into the sack together the next. He's got everything a marriage has except the piece of paper to make it legal."

Edge was on the brink of sleep, unconcerned with the sounds from the wagon, which merged with the almost hypnotic regularity of the distant crash of ocean breakers. But Case's voice drew him back to full awareness and he heard the clop of hooves and rattle of turning wheels. He craned his neck to look around the cooking pot on the fire and saw Clarence French's buggy approaching camp along the logging trail. But then the fat man veered the white horse to one side, steering around behind the arc of parked wagons. The moonlight filtering through the high redwoods shone on the gold-plating of one of his six-guns. The buggy did not stop, but picked up the trail again beyond the camp and continued south at a gentle pace.

In watching the buggy emerge from behind the wagons, Edge caught sight of a figure standing in the moon shade of a tree: surreptitiously until the white gelding had hauled the fat man out of sight. Then the figure moved to climb into a wagon and the half-breed saw the thrusting breasts and flared hips which marked the watcher as a woman. Moonlight striking blonde hair identified her as Jo Jo Lamont.

"I hear it doesn't work out that way for Turk and his target," Edge said as he stretched out full length beneath his blankets again.

"She claims she's still pure," Case replied lazily, sighing again now that a full two minutes had passed without interruption by laughter.

"Now you settled Turk's hash, they still got a show," Grainger growled, and gave a short, harsh laugh of his own. "Just need a new sign, that's all." He moved his hand in the air, as if it helped him to visualize the lettering. "See the only virgin west of the Mississippi."

Nobody else expressed amusement and the almost complete silence settled over the clearing again, marred only by the ocean, the crackle of fires and the

54

deep breathing and occasional snores of the sleepers. Edge's mind, accustomed to these sounds, reacted to the intrusion of another and snapped him awake the instant it made itself heard. He had slept with his right hand curled around the butt of the Colt. As his eyes cracked open, his fingers tightened, one of them pressing against the trigger. His thumb rested on the hammer.

"Reflexes like an animal," Salter hissed sourly.

The sound which had roused the half-breed was of the guard's footfalls. Or perhaps it wasn't this at all. Maybe the merest vibration of the ground upon which the big man trod: or just an ever-alert mind responding to the warning of a sixth sense. Whatever it was, the dark-eyed young guard with a broken nose and a knife-scar on his cheek had come as close to explaining the result as anybody could get. Had there been the slightest hint of an attack in his attitude, the Colt would have exploded death an instant after the half-breed's eyes opened. But Salter had the Winchester slung under an arm and his hand was rubbing his chin, far from the holstered revolver.

Edge curled back his lips in a cold grin as he sat up. "Sense of smell to match, feller," he muttered. "Appreciate it if next time you get close to me, you'd stay on the downwind side."

On the other side of the fire, Wylie was rousing Grainger. It took a lot longer and the eldest guard came awake with a string of mixed grunts and curses. Salter confined his response to a soured look and backed away as Edge stood up, putting on his hat, strapping the gunbelt around his waist and slanting the rifle across his shoulder.

"Midnight, Roy," Wylie told the ill-tempered man. "You and the new guy now."

"So don't sound so goddamn pleased about it,"

55

Grainger growled, giving Edge a fish-eyed look across the fire.

Then the flames leapt higher as Salter tossed new kindling on the embers. The salty air was a lot colder now as it streamed off the ocean and curled through the redwoods. Edge took one of his recent purchases out of his gear pouch. A fur-lined jacket, cut short enough so that it didn't cover his holster. He shrugged into it as he moved to the wagon. He was tall enough to look over the tailgate without dropping it. The flare of a match danced in reflection on the smooth yellow metal.

"You don't trust Wylie and Salter?" Grainger snorted, crooking his Winchester under his arm and blowing on his cupped hands.

"Only one person I trust," the half-breed answered.

"Who's that?"

"Me."

Grainger spat. "Stupid of me to ask."

"Nobody's perfect," Edge told him, and began to amble in a full circle around the wagon.

Grainger leaned against the tailgate and began to roll a cigarette. He had time to light it and smoke it halfway down before Edge returned.

"Enjoy the moonlight stroll?" he asked.

"Wasn't for the exercise."

"For what?"

"Checking ways the gold can get taken."

Grainger scowled. "Ain't no way, lessen they cream us, hitch the team and drive the wagon outta camp."

Edge nodded. "Right feller. So I'll see you in the morning."

"Hey!" Grainger called after him, keeping his voice low. "Where you goin'?"

"Get me a decent night's sleep in a real bed for a

56

change. Not a chance in a million anyone's going to make a try while we're camped."

He looked over his shoulder to reply to Grainger, and shot several more glances in that direction as he crossed the campsite to where the logging trail cut through the trees towards town. Grainger stared after him in confusion for awhile, then shrugged and leaned against a rear wheel to enjoy his cigarette. Just before Edge went on to the trail through the trees, he thought he glimpsed moonlight shining on the guard's teeth. But the man's hat brim shadowed the rest of his face and it was impossible to tell whether he was smiling or sneering.

The half-breed trod lightly and knew that when he was out of sight of the camp, he was also beyond earshot. Then he angled off the trail and his gait changed from ambling to striding. There was little brush amongst the thick, towering trunks of the giant redwoods. Mostly the forest was floored with grass, moss and the rotted leaves of countless falls. But though his stride was lengthened, he continued to set his feet down lightly, conscious that a dry twig might be concealed by the dead leaves or the grass beneath each lowered boot.

He moved silently away from the trail on a right-angled course for about three hundred feet, then turned again, to head back the way he had come. Nearing the camp, he saw the occasional crimson glow of a fire. Once, from a distance of about a hundred and fifty feet, he saw the end of the wagon between a natural avenue of trees: clearly silhouetted against a fire. He saw Grainger, too, squatting down with his back resting against the rim of a rearwheel. But the half-breed didn't stop. He continued silently in a southern direction for a few more feet, then swung towards the ocean.

He reached the continuation of the logging trail some thirty feet down from where it led out of the clearing on the far side from Seascape. It curved a little on this side and he had to backtrack again to find a point from which he could watch the wagon containing the big gold. Here, the absence of brush was a disadvantage. For he could only use a thick redwood trunk for cover and it was possible that a keen-eyed watcher might spot him each time he peered around the ridged bark to survey the clearing.

But nobody did and, as the night grew older and colder, a grey and damp mist rolling in from the Pacific to hover eerily amid the forest, he began to think that he might have guessed wrong. But he felt no sense of frustration. He was being paid well and was allowed to do the job the way he wanted. He asked for nothing else and neither did he expect it. Fate called the pattern of every man's life. All the man could do was watch for the new piece to be slotted into place and be ready to use it for his own ends.

They started to steal the big gold at two o'clock by Edge's reckoning. Grainger didn't have to rouse Wylie and Salter. All that was necessary to get them from under their blankets was a low whistle. And after they had got to their feet and stepped lightly over to the wagon, there was no exchange of words. Not even hand signals. The plan to steal the wagon had obviously been well rehearsed.

Only in cutting four horses out of the remuda did Wylie and Salter make any sound, whispering softly and placatingly to keep the animals calm. The horses knew the scent of the men and there was no disturbance as they were led into position to be harnessed to the wagon. Grainger had moved to the side, taking his role of guard more seriously now. But the Winchester he held across the front of his broad chest was this time ready to swing into covering the people sleeping in the camp.

No matter how quiet men remain, and are able to persuade their animals to be, a four horse team cannot be hitched up in absolute silence. Shod hooves thudded against turf, bones cracked, harness slapped and horses snorted. Normal, everyday sounds. But in the dead of a misty night they had a strangely loud quality. There had to be at least one light sleeper among the score or more people sprawled under blankets beside the fires or slumbering in the wagons. But nobody woke. And though Wylie and Salter did their chores with a sense of urgency, there was also a certain brash confidence in their actions. Grainger, too, despite the steady rifle, showed almost careless nonchalance as he swung his head from side to side, surveying the camp.

Then, as the two younger guards returned to the remuda and saddled three horses, Edge remembered Case drinking the coffee. And he also recalled that Grainger had been at a campfire which wasn't his own when the dude and the half-breed returned from town. Edge had not drunk any coffee after eating the stew.

Not that it mattered. Edge was the only man in the camp being paid to protect the big gold from its guards. And his plan to do it did not involve getting help from anybody else.

One of the saddle horses was hitched to the rear of the wagon. Grainger and Salter mounted the other two. Wylie hoisted himself up on to the wagon seat. Now there was a signal: a curt nod of the head by Grainger. He and Salter turned their horses and Winchesters towards the camp. Wylie unwound the reins from around the brake lever.

"Giiiiittttt uppppp there!" he yelled, and snatched

59

a whip from the seat to lash across the backs of the team.

The animals whinnied in alarm, then reared and lunged forward. The tendons stood out on their hindquarters, and then the initial effort of setting the great weight rolling was over. The wheels rose up out of the dents they had sunk into the turf, and the wagon was moving.

Somebody shouted something from the far side of the camp. A man. Walter Peat who had had other things on his mind besides coffee when he brought Arabella back from Seascape? Or one of the spielers who had also been late into camp?

"Shut your mouth and go to sleep!" Grainger yelled.

Wylie continued to whip the horses and started to scream a string of obscenities at them in demand for greater speed. He was yanking on the reins, steering the team towards the start of the trail beside which Edge waited. It hadn't been difficult to call the direction the thieves would take. Town lay to the north. And Clarence French had driven his buggy south.

Salter sent a shot towards the wagons, the bullet cracking across the campsite and thudding into something metal. The impact sounded more stridently loud than the report.

"Lunkhead!" Grainger snarled, jerking on his reins to order the horse into a wheel before thudding his heels for a gallop in pursuit of the wagon.

Salter was only a yard behind him as more shots rang out and figures sprang up at the firesides. Forms that swayed, reeled and even collapsed again. The wagon kept up its headlong pace, displacing tendrils of white mist that swirled around it like smoke from wet wood smouldering without flames. Edge had been crouched behind the tree. Now he stood up to his full height, the metallic scraping of the rifle's lever action lost amid so much other raucous sound. He stayed in cover, except for one side of his face as he peered out around the rough bark.

Wylie had to haul the team into another turn to get on to the logging trail. A sharper one this time, in the opposite direction to the first. A left hand turn that put most of the dragging strain on to the offside wheels. Edge was positioned on the left of the trail. He saw the wagon canting to the right while Wylie leaned to the other side. He watched the front offside wheel wobble, then spin at a faster rate as it came clear of the ground. It slammed down into the turf again, bounced, and spun free. It quivered through the air with the power of a catapulted missile, then its iron rim dug a massive piece of bark from a tree trunk. The front axle bit into the ground, half stopping the hurtling wagon. Then it snapped. The front of the wagon's chassis scraped an enormous black scar across the lush turf. The rear of the wagon skewed into a side-slid, started to tip, and then smashed into a tree. The two lead horses broke from the traces to bolt while the back pair were stopped dead in their tracks. They reared, snorting in pain and terror. Wylie was pitched from his seat and his scream cut clearly across every other sound of the wreck. The splintering of wood, the grating of gold against iron, the fear and pain of the horses and the impact of wagon into tree.

The power of his involuntary motion snapped the reins from his hands and he turned head-over-heels in a graceful arc. The short trajectory sailed him between the necks of the rearing horses and thudded him into the ground at the base of a tree. His screams ended in a deep-throated groan as Edge stepped out from behind the tree.

A handgun began to crack. A small calibre weapon, the sounds of its reports diminished by the cacophony which had preceded them.

"Let's get outta here, Ray!" The voice was recognizable as that of Salter.

"But for you, we'd have made it!" Wylie gasped.

Edge glanced down at the man on the ground. His feet had hit first. At an awkward angle. Both legs had broken at the ankles. His feet had been wrenched off by the impact and thrown across the trail. Shards of broken bone showed up incredibly white against the rivers of blood flowing from the meaty stumps. He had lost both his rifle and his handgun during the rapid ejection from the wagon seat. Not that he could have used them. His hands were turned at acute angles from his fractured wrists.

"Lot of gold to lose, feller," the half-breed muttered. "Natural you're broken up about it."

"How?" Wylie croaked.

"For two pins, I'll tell you." He dropped the metal retaining pins he had taken from the front wheel hubs of the wagon. They splashed into Wylie's blood.

Then he whirled, slamming the Winchester against his shoulder. He squeezed the trigger and missed the target. The wrecked wagon was almost completely blocking the trail. Grainger had chosen the escape route, angling across the campsite and into the timber at the southeast corner of the clearing. But Salter was a little late in chasing after the older man, and there was an instant for a clear shot as he galloped across the narrow gap between the canting wagon and the trees flanking the trail. The man with the light handgun got him first. Winging him in the thigh. Salter instinctively leaned forward to claw at the place where he had been hit. The bullet from the Winchester cracked across the back of the man's neck. Then he was lost to sight, the hoofbeats of his mount diminishing. There were no more shots.

"Goddamn gun's empty!" Roger Case shrieked in high-pitched anger. "Blast at them, somebody."

"Ain' our gold they was after!" a man snorted in response.

"Edge! Where the hell are you, Edge?" The dude's voice seemed to have risen an octave, quivering close to hysteria.

"Maybe they killed the bastard, I hope!"

The hoofbeats had almost faded into nothing now as Grainger and Salter put distance between themselves and the scene of their abortive attempt to steal the big gold. The words rang out clearly in the misty night. Weak as it was, the half-breed recognized the voice of Turk.

"Ain't your day, feller!" he called evenly.

"Oh, Christ!" Jo Jo Lamont groaned.

"Oh, dear, dear me!" The Nepalese put in.

"Edge!" Case yelled, relief dragging his voice down to a normal level. He started to run drunkenly towards the wrecked wagon. "What happened to Wylie? You see him?"

"Yeah," the half-breed replied sardonically. "But nobody'll be seeing so much of him again."

"What's that supposed to mean?"

Case had reached the gap between the wreck and the trees. He saw Wylie and stopped abruptly. His pale face shaded whiter and the skin took on a sheen. A wet gurgle vented from his lips. A pepperbox dropped from his hand.

Edge shouldered the Winchester. "Means he's lost a couple of feet."

CHAPTER FIVE

"What's your name, feller?" Edge asked.

The Nepalese came awake with a start, sat up sharply and banged his forehead painfully against the axle of the wagon under which he had been sleeping. He yelled, and the two tigers growled irritably.

"Oh, goodness gracious me!" he exclaimed, his dark eyes growing wide in his brown face. "You frightened me most badly."

The half-breed was squatting down at the side of the wagon, a menacing silhouette against the white sea mist which had thickened as the early hours of the new day past. Visibility was down to just a few feet and the fires which could be seen were mere ghostly orange glows suspended in the murk.

"No sweat," Edge said softly. "What's your name?"

The small, wiry-built Nepalese massaged his forehead. "Vishwabandhu Nageshwar Singh, sahib," he replied nervously.

64

Edge pursed his lips. "Guess that's why you get called Nep."

The man looked said. "I like to be called Singh best, sahib. But if you prefer, I am not a man of violence. You will call me what you will, most certainly."

"Need your help, Singh."

His teeth were whiter than the mist against his dark complexion. "Most pleased I will be, sahib."

"Case'll pay you the eight dollars a day."

Singh's grin broadened. "Mr. Case is indeed a most generous man."

"He don't know it yet," Edge said flatly. "Thinks he's saving that much now he's light four guards."

Perhaps he was, in his sleep. Grainger *had* made a circuit of the camp fires the previous night, dropping some kind of soporific drug into the coffee pots. It was apparent in the way all but a handful of the showmen and spielers went quickly back to sleep after the violent disturbance of the attempt to steal the big gold.

Walter Peat and another man who had not drunk any of the doped coffee carried the critically injured Wylie to Doc Elkins' office in Seascape. But the man had lost too much blood and a lot more drained from the stumps of his ankles on the jolting trip to town. He died on the way, cursing Edge, and was taken to the funeral parlor instead.

Once he was assured that the block of precious metal was safe, Case surrendered again to the effects of the Mickey Finn and crawled gratefully back under his blankets. And even those who had not been drugged returned quickly to their makeshift beds after surveying the wreckage. It became even more apparent that the dude's crowd-pulling exhibit was resented by the other carny people, who relished the fact that it looked like the end of the trail for the customer-cornering big gold.

Edge waited for an hour beside one of the larger fires, drinking coffee freshly made in his own pot and smoking two cigarettes. Then he went to rouse the Nepalese. The camp was even quieter than before, uncomfortably damp sea mist having a muffling effect on the slight sounds which did disturb the tranquil early morning hours. Then, after getting the willing co-operation of Singh, more sound invaded the clearing. The snorts of horses, the growls of wilder animals, the creaking of ropes under heavy strain, the grunts of laboring men and the mournful music of the harmonica.

The job took three hours to complete and for a lot of the time the half-breed and the Nepalese were unaware of the chill of approaching dawn as they heaved, pulled and sweated at their work. Sometimes a weary voice called for quiet, but Edge and Singh ignored the demands and nobody came to see what was happening. The mist was whiter when it was over, for the first greyness of the new day was creeping in from the east, pushing the night's darkness out over the ocean.

"We get some sleep now, I think will be most good idea," Singh suggested with a yawn rubbing his aching muscles.

Edge grinned. "Just don't snore, feller."

He disappeared into the mist and Singh, bewildered, bedded down beneath the wagon again. He had hardly had time to close his eyes before the half-breed reappeared, hauling his bedroll.

"To have the company I am most pleased, sahib."

"Saying it's good enough," the half-breed growled as he ducked under the wagon and unfurled the bedroll beside Singh's gear.

66

The Nepalese showed his sparkling white teeth. "Back home in Katmandu I have one wife and eight children, sahib. In San Francisco there is most high-born Indian girl who is with child by fruit of my loins. I am most certainly not to pansy boy. Oh dear, dear me, no. My taste is indeed for passion-flowers."

"Keep it that way," Edge said, tipping his hat over his eyes. "And you'll still have a stalk to get fuity with."

The camp came awake slowly and irritably. The traumatic interruption to drugged sleep had the effect of lengthening the period it took to shake off the heavy-eyed drowsiness of most of the carny people. The sun was high and hot enough to have burned off the final traces of mist by the time the majority of the people camped in the clearing became fully aware of their surroundings. Case was one of the last to wake up.

Shaking his head to clear the fuzziness that clouded his mind and blurred his vision, he dressed hurriedly and went to survey the wreckage of his wagon. The first doubts hit him when he failed to see Edge standing guard on the wreckage. Then he saw that the wagon had suffered further disintegration after the crash. The rear wheels had been removed, the side canvas was torn and the side board was missing.

"Edge!" he yelled. Then, when he drew aside the ripped canvas with a trembling hand, his voice rose to the pitch of hysteria it had reached the previous night. "Edge, it's gone! The gold's gone!"

People halted their preparations for breakfast and stared towards the slight form of the near-demented dude. Case whirled, drawing wide the canvas.

"Look, for Christsake!" he screamed. "It's gone." Blood vessels stood out like lengths of blue cord against his pale features. "The whole goddamn inside of the goddamn wagon." He tried to say more, but his throat constricted, trapping the words inside him.

Nobody moved in for a closer look.

"We all got our problems, Case," the man billed as the rubber man called gleefully. "I just cooked me an egg and it's bad."

"Bastards!" Case roared as laughter rippled around the campsite.

"Quit yelling, feller!" the half-breed called evenly, and the noise quietened as he rose from the wagon, stretching.

"Where's my goddamn gold?" Case roared, and delved a hand under his jacket.

The half-breed's arms had been reaching far out to the sides as he flexed his muscles after the short sleep. They swept down to his body in a blur of speed, the right hand draping the butt of the Colt. "Don't do it, feller!" he snapped. "Last time I saw that peashooter, it was empty. But you point it at me, I'll kill you anyway."

Case stayed his hand.

"Most wise indeed, Mr. Case, sahib," Singh announced, stepping lithely out to stand beside Edge. "I show him, Edge sahib?"

Edge sighed. "You don't, he's liable to bust something fatal."

Nodding enthusiastically, the Nepalese clambered up on to the seat of his wagon, then went higher, on to the flat roof. Dramatically, Singh hauled at the canvas cover. The tigers roared, baring their massive teeth as they blinked into the sunlight. The teeth were yellow. But not so yellow as the block of gold that was set solidly in the center of the wagon bed. The striped animals had been squatting on their haunches one on each side of the big gold—like trained sentries. Now they continued to play their unwitting roles. With growls quivering from their jaws, and tails swishing with menace, the animals rose and began to move. Prowling in a circle in the restricted area between the gold block and the iron bars of the cage built on to the wagon.

The carny people stared in silent awe at the spectacle. Edge relaxed into nonchalance and stooped to gather up his gear. Singh squatted proudly atop the cage, arms folded and a broad grin pasted on his dark features. But the dude's expression was even brighter as he launched into a run and skidded to a halt beside the cage wagon. One of the wild beasts prodded a paw through the bars, claws extended in an attempted maul. But Case seemed totally unaware that he was only an inch or so out of range. His wide eyes drank in the sight of his gold, securely held upon the iron framework taken from the wrecked wagon.

"How on earth did you manage it?" he gasped at length.

"Wasn't easy," Edge replied wryly.

"I was great help, indeed yes," Singh announced, and dropped the canvas back to veil the cage at a nod from the half-breed.

"Right," Edge agreed. "And he's on the payroll."

His panic over, Case became the hard-headed businessman again. "I do my own hiring, Edge!" he snapped.

"After last night, that's something you shouldn't boast about," the half-breed told him evenly. "Singh's getting eight bucks a day, same as you were paying Grainger and his partners."

The dude seemed on the point of exploding into anger, but he held it back. "I'll think about it," he said tensely.

"Figured you would. And thinking's best done like a lot of other things—on a full stomach."

With his own wagon wrecked, Case loaded his gear onto Singh's cage vehicle after breakfast. Everyone attached to the carny helped to move the wreckage off the logging trail, for until it was cleared there was no way south for anyone. Edge was the only man with a saddle horse to ride and he rode it several hundred feet ahead of the train. Not to scout the way, for such a chore was unnecessary. The narrow track cut through the timber for about a mile, curving to the left and right by turns and then broadened into a trail proper after swinging past a sawmill. Today was Monday but it was still early morning and there was only one man at the mill. Smoke curled from the chimney of a small shack at the side of the larger building and the man was sitting in the doorway, drinking coffee, smoking a pipe and contemplating a distant patch of blue that was the ocean viewed between the brows of two hills. He was an old man with skin like cracked leather, and no teeth.

"You live here?" Edge asked, reining the stallion to a halt.

"All the time. Nightwatchman when it's dark. Fix the boys their food in the daytime."

"Have any visitors last night?"

The old man sucked wetly on the pipe. "Seascape Lumber Company don't pay me much, mister. Information'll cost you a dollar."

Edge swung easily out of the saddle. "Cost you a fat lip if you don't give it to me, feller."

The old timer pressed himself hard against the back of his chair. "You wouldn't hit an old guy like me, mister!"

Edge swung his head and narrowed his eyes to glinting slits to look towards the distant ocean. "Tell you what I'll do. I'll give you the dollar; you bet

70

me I wouldn't smack you in the mouth; and I'll win it back."

He turned to survey the old timer and the blueness beneath his hooded lids was brighter than that of the Pacific. It looked a lot colder and a lot deeper, too.

The old timer swallowed hard. "Not visitors, mister. Guy went by in a buggy. Big fat guy. I ain't never seen a guy so fat. White horse. Then later—two or three hours—a couple of riders. Moving fast. Like they had bullets up their asses and the lead was still hot." He squinted his weak eyes and saw the hardness had retreated from the surface of the half-breed's weathered features. "Ain't that worth nothin', mister?"

Edge could hear the rattling of the approaching wagons as they trundled down the logging trail. He swung back up into the saddle. "Sure is. My appreciation."

"I can't put that in my pipe and smoke it!" the old timer yelled irritably after the departing rider.

"Quit smoking and live longer."

"I'll be ninety-seven day after tomorrow!"

"So die."

He returned his attention to the ground, which was dustier out from under the trees, and retained sign better than the logging trail. There had been too much traffic in the immediate vicinity of the sawmill for anything to be learned from the wheeltracks and hoofprints. But further south, as the trail swung towards the coast, it had been used less recently. The sign left by the buggy and the single horse in its shafts were plain to see: overstamped by the hoofprints of two saddle horses. As the morning progressed, the sun's heat seeming to increase with every passing minute, the half-breed dropped back to stay closer to the lead wagon of the train. This was the one carrying the gold and the tigers: Singh taking the reins and Case sitting up on the seat beside him. The dude wore a neckerchief like a bandit's mask over his mouth and nostrils. But his eyes stayed screwed up and his forehead remained lined in a constant grimace: for the silk fabric was unable to completely combat the stench of tiger wet and droppings that emanated from under the canvas cover.

Because of the foul miasma, which clung to the cage wagon like an invisible cloud, the second vehicle in the train maintained a wide gap to its rear. Edge was far enough ahead to be out of range, except when an infrequent air current leapt off the ocean to grasp and spread the smell. Familiarity with bad odor, or a diminished sense of smell, left the Nepalese unmoved by the noisome nuisance caused by his animals. He either rode in the wagon in beaming contentment, or serenaded the tigers with his harmonica.

Timber grew in isolated stands now and for the most part the trail cut through, or curved over, low hills. The ground was covered by tough brush which leaned to the east, witnessing the strength of the ocean winds that powered inland during the winter months. But winter seemed a long way off on this day, when the sky competed with the ocean for a depth of blueness and the sun blazed so fiercely it seemed about to evaporate the vast expanse of water. The terrain had been steadily sloping towards sea level all morning and it was little after midday when the half-breed spotted traces of a small camp.

A narrow stream meandered down from the hills, cut across the trail and emptied into a rocky pool that would be submerged by salt water at high tide. The grey and black ashes of a fire, long out, were spread at the side of the trail where it was crossed by the stream. A half-dozen cigarette stubs were nearby.

Other signs showed clearly where the buggy had been parked, the shafts leaning into the ground after the gelding had been unhitched from the harness. There were the tracks of two more horses close to where a patch of brush had been foraged for meagre food. And the dust held the impressions where three men had rested. Deep tracks across the soft sand suggested Clarence French had taken a dip in the ocean before moving out along the trail again, escorted by Grainger and Salter.

"The men who try to steal the big gold camped here, sahib?" Singh asked as he rolled the cage wagon to a halt short of fording the narrow stream.

"Picked a good place," Edge answered, sliding from the saddle and then stretching out full length to drink some water a couple of feet upstream from where the stallion was sucking in refreshment.

"You park that rig there!" Walter Peat yelled, swinging his wagon around the stalled one and splashing across the stream.

The other vehicles in the train took the same line and rolled to a halt in a long arc just off the trail three hundred feet south. Case watched them enviously as men and women leapt to the ground and began to gather brush for cooking fires.

"You think Grainger and Salter might try again, Edge?" he asked.

"They're heading the same way as we are," the half-breed pointed out. "But then there aren't any other trails a buggy could take but this one."

"Buggy?" The dude was bewildered. Then it hit him. "The fat man—French—is involved?"

"Build a fire, Singh," Edge instructed, and the little Nepalese went to work eagerly. The lean half-breed nodded. "Looks like. Seemed to me he knew Dana Breeze in the saloon last night. And he got a

73

little hot under the collar when Breeze started to make trouble. Then he headed out of town a couple of hours before they tried to knock off your gold." He spat into the dead embers of the old fire as Singh built a new one. "And the three of them tied up here and then lit out together."

Case thought about the evidence, and for awhile it disturbed him more than the evil smell from in back of him. Then he reached a decision, and clambered down from the wagon, dragging the mask off his lower face.

"So you'd better keep a sharp look out for trouble," he ordered. "That's what I'm paying you for. I don't have to suffer this obnoxious stink while I'm eating lunch."

This said, he hiked up his pants cuffs to keep them dry and waded the stream to go to join the main body of the carny transport. Singh watched the retreating figure, dusting himself down as he walked.

"I am very pleased indeed that you do not find the odor of my most magnificent beasts unpleasant, sahib," he said to the half-breed as he set a match to the kindling.

"I think they stink to high heaven, feller," Edge replied.

"But you will stay to share the repast with me, I hope very much indeed."

"I slept with the stink, I guess I can eat with it."

"I cook most fine beef curry for sahib?" He grinned. "I most fine cook."

"Do that," Edge told him, looking across the stream to where a figure had broken from one of the groups around a fire and was walking back along the trail. The full figure of Jo Jo Lamont, today dressed in a modest, high-necked gown of plain white. She carried a pitcher to get water from the stream and walked with her eyes gazing down at the ground, to avoid meeting the half-breed's cool stare. He waited until she had crouched at the bank and submerged the pitcher. Then he drew the Colt, cocking the hammer as the barrel cleared the holster.

She saw the image of his actions in reflection on the sun-shimmered surface of the stream. A gasp escaped her lips. She started to rise. Edge squeezed the trigger and she screamed, falling backwards to sit down hard. The bullet hissed into the water and clanged against the metal pitcher. It bored a hole in either side and then buried itself into the streambed.

"Why the hell did you do that?" she shrieked at him.

Singh had looked up in alarm at the shot. Then he shrugged and continued with the cooking chore, chanting in his native language as the tigers growled and rocked the wagon. Shocked faces looked towards the stream from where the other wagons were parked.

"Get your attention," Edge replied evenly.

"My name's Miss Lamont," she snapped, getting up on to her haunches and snatching the pitcher out of the stream. She stood up, her eyes blazing malevolently across the water. "You could have just said that."

Edge nodded. "Miss Lamont?"

"Yes!"

"You're getting another dress all wet."

She looked down at herself. The entry and exit holes of the bullet were on the same curving side of the pitcher. Spouts of water arced out of both of them to drench the full skirt of her dress.

"Oh, you beast!" she rasped, and hurled the pitcher into the stream. She whirled and made to run back to the main camp.

The Colt bucked in Edge's hand. Four times. The

75

girl froze, sideways on to the half-breed, covering her ears with her hands and trembling from head to toe. Two bullets tossed up divots of dirt in front of her and two behind her.

"Wasn't your bad luck with water I wanted to talk to you about," Edge said. "And I've saved one bullet in this gun in case you don't tell me what I want to hear."

She had moved her hands away from her ears to cradle her cheeks. Her long, painted nails dug into the flesh beneath her tightly closed eyes as she struggled to control her trembling.

"Please, sahib!" Singh implored. "I would most humbly beg you not to shoot the gun no more. My tigers, they very much do not like it."

The wagon was rocking frenetically as the two wild beasts prowled around the rich freight and vented deep-throated roars of anger.

"Play one of your sad tunes to them, feller," Edge suggested. "Might help Miss Lamont to sing."

The Nepalese already had the harmonica to his lips. The moment Edge was finished, he began to make music with it, marching anxiously around the wagon as the plaintive notes drifted through the hot air.

"What do you want from me?" the girl pleaded, her voice anguished.

"You were up and about when the fat man left Seascape last night," the half-breed said evenly as the volume of the tigers' anger subsided. "Out at the side of the clearing where the logging trail cut south."

Her shattered nerves were calming: as if Singh's mournful music had the same effect on her as it did on the tigers. Her trembling had stopped and after a few moments she was able to let her hands fall to her sides. There were vivid red marks beneath her eyes where the fingernails had left their impressions. She

76

hung her head to avoid meeting the half-breed's hooded stare when she turned towards the stream.

"I swear to God I'm going to tell you the truth," she said hoarsely.

"You'll be able to do it in person if you don't," he answered. "Providing it's true that all virgins got a free pass."

The girl gave a deep sigh and continued to gaze down at her own reflection in the stream. "That was the truth, what I told you last night. I'm deeply ashamed."

"Tell some more truth and I'll give you the gun so you can shoot yourself," Edge invited.

She looked up at him then, to show him the tears crawling from the corners of her eyes and coursing down her cheeks. "Please, I'm desperate. And you are the cause. Try to understand."

He didn't answer and she drew in a deep breath. "I'm a good girl, but I want a good life. Turk said he'd pay me well for helping him with his show. Maybe he would have, if we'd got to San Francisco and he still had his show. I was so mad at you . . . that's why I tried to kill you."

"I know that part," Edge told her as Singh succeeded in calming the tigers and returned to the fire. "I was there."

"Then I offered to let you . . . you know."

Edge pursed his lips. "I was there that time, as well." His impatience showed in a further narrowing of his eyes, which looked like slivers of ice against the burnished flesh of his face.

"It gave me the idea. The fat man kept looking at me in Seascape. From the time we arrived he just didn't seem able to take his eyes off me. I knew he wanted to . . . you know?" She colored and stared into the stream again. "Well, I got to thinking. Being

77

a . . . you know? Well, it ain't something really special is it. So I figured I'd trade it. The fat man wears good clothes and carries them fancy guns—drives an expensive buggy with a fine horse. It looked like he was rich."

The harshness left the half-breed's lean features and he curled back his lips to bare his teeth. "So you reckoned it was time you made use of your hole card."

"Must you be so crude?" she demanded, brushing the tears from her cheeks.

Edge tipped up the Colt and turned the cylinder to eject the spent shells. He started to reload fresh ammunition from his belt.

"He just rode right on by me," Jo Jo said sulkily. "Just scowled at me and went on his way. Twice in one night I shamed myself. And for what? Nothing?"

"You still got something," the half-breed told her evenly. "But right now Singh's curry is the only hot stuff that appeals to me."

Jo Jo stabbed a withering look at him through her tears and whirled. She ran back to where the wagons were parked, feet kicking up dust to cling to the damp patches on her dress.

"You believe the most distressed lady, sahib?" Singh asked as he stirred the cooking pot.

"I reckon," Edge replied softly, catching sight of something which moved at the brow of one of the brush-covered hills through which the stream flowed. "What would she want with just a share of a ton and a half of the stuff . . ."

He whirled and powered into a crouched run, curling out his free arm. The Nepalese gave a shriek of alarm as he was snatched bodily from the ground. He was carried, writhing, across six feet of open ground and then flung beneath the wagon. His head cracked against an axle again and he thought the

78

explosion was inside his own head. But then, as Edge thudded down beside him and snatched up the Winchester, he saw the stallion drop into a kneel and then topple sideways. Blood gushed in a vivid fountain from the hole where the animal's left eye had been. It looked like smoke billowing in the stream water.

The half-breed worked the rifle's lever action and completed his sentence against a background of further shots: "When she's just found out she's sitting on a gold mine."

CHAPTER SIX

"Oh dear, dear Me!" Singh exclaimed, pushing his face hard against the ground and covering the back of his head with his hands. "I have no wish to die here."

The movement Edge had seen was that of a polished rifle barrel as it swung to the aim and the sun glinted on it. But after that first shot which had killed the stallion instead of him, there was more than just a rifle to see. Eight men crested the brow of the hill. Seven were already mounted and the eighth, who had been prone in the brush to fire the opening shot, swung up into the saddle of a horse led by one of the other men.

Now they galloped down the hillside in line abreast. Grainger and Salter were on the flanks, controlling their horses with heels and knees, prairie Indian fashion, as they used both hands to fire their Winchesters. One man rode with the reins gripped between his teeth as he blasted down the slope with matched six-guns. The others were less skilled riders, firing past the necks of their animals with repeating rifles while keeping a firm grip on the reins.

"So get 'em before they get you!" Edge rasped, using his elbow to push the discarded Colt towards the cowering Singh.

Bullets were thudding into the ground and the wagon. Wilder shots clanged against the cooking pot, showered sparks from the fire and splashed into the stream. Edge drew a bead on Salter, whose left pants leg was crusted with dried blood from where Case had winged him. He squeezed the trigger and fresh blood erupted. From the chest, left of center. The man died in the saddle and fell backwards over the hindquarters of his horse. The animal, frightened by the thud of the dead weight against his rump, veered suddenly to one side. It slammed hard into the flank of the next horse in line. This was ridden by the man with the reins in his teeth. As his mount leaned, he dropped his revolvers and tried to keep his balance. But the angle of tilt was too great. He fell to the side, one foot slipping free of the stirrup. But the other was held firm. He crashed to the ground with a scream that spurted his horse to greater effort. He was dragged at breakneck speed on his back.

"I friggin' missed!" Grainger yelled, and snatched up the reins to haul his horse into a wheel.

"I am most non-violent Nepalese," Singh shrieked as a bullet ricochetted off a wheel rim and spat dirt into his hair.

The tigers were roaring in fear and anger, rocking the wagon frantically as they chased around the big gold. The team stood in docile immobility in the traces. Familiar with the tantrums of the wild beasts, they were also immune to the explosive cracking of gunfire.

"More men die for ideals than anything else!" the

half-breed rasped. He fired again, as the five other attackers still in their saddles turned to stream after Grainger.

The man being dragged was plunged into the stream and became lost to sight amid the spray raised by pumping hooves and the aquaplaning of his own body. Diluted blood colored the white water of his wake. Edge's second shot took a man in the side of the head, and a dying nerve spasm sent him rigidly upright in the stirrups before he toppled to the side, trailing an arc of blood from his ear.

The men concentrated on retreat, yelling at their mounts and slamming in their heels to drive the horses back up the slope. They were no longer firing. But a new source of gunfire opened up. The pathetically insignificant crackle of the pepperbox and the much more forceful reports of a repeating rifle.

Edge snatched a look across the stream, over the hump of the inert form of the man who had been snatched free of the stirrup. Case and Jo Jo Lamont had sprinted away from the wagons and had reached the bank of the water course. The dude was standing erect, in the formal stance of a duellist, methodically firing the tiny gun across a hopeless range. The girl was prone on the ground beside him, elbows firm into the dirt, cheek against the stock and blazing away at the attackers like somebody born with a Winchester in their hands.

When the half-breed's eyes swung back to look up the rise, their faintly amused expression changed to one of guarded admiration. The girl had already blasted one man from the saddle. Another slumped forward and thudded to the ground as Edge drew a bead on him.

The three survivors, leaning into the necks of their straining mounts, reached the brow of the hill. Edge raked the rifle barrel across the backs of two of them and zeroed in on the nape of Grainger's neck just as the riders started down the far slope. The girl had selected the same man for a target and the two rifles exploded simultaneously. Grainger's head seemed to disintegrate in a shower of torn flesh, spraying blood and shattered bone. But the crest of the hill hid his fall. And the two survivors were screened from further shots.

"My life is indeed owed to you, sahib!" Singh croaked, raising his head and cracking his fingers to peer between them at the crumpled forms littering the slope. "What a pity you had to use such violent means to save it."

"They didn't seem ready to be talked out of blasting you, feller," the half-breed muttered, snatching up the Colt and scrambling out from under the wagon.

The tigers were still venting fierce roars as they bounded about inside the wagon. Edge didn't even bother to check the stallion with its blood-run head covered with feeding flies. As he leapt up on to the wagon seat, he caught a glimpse of Case and Jo Jo Lamont, looking towards him with wide eyes staring out of pale, shocked faces. And beyond them he saw the rest of the carny showmen and spielers, continuing with preparations for their midday meal as if the attack had never happened.

Then he kicked off the brake lever and slapped the reins across the backs of the team, yelling at the horses to urge them into movement. They responded immediately, as if the sounds of the battle and the scent of blood and cordite in their nostrils had been building up a powerful reserve of strength in them while they stood in obedient and unmoving silence. Now they unleashed it, swinging into a tight turn at

83

the dictates of the reins. Snorts vented from quivering nostrils.

"Edge!" Case yelled, and seemed rooted to the spot.

"Goodness gracious, my beautiful beasts!" Singh had started to rise, then pitched out full-length again as the heavily-laden wagon jerked forward. One of the wheels missed his hand-covered head by an inch. Then, once he felt the sun beating down on him, he jumped upright, sprinted in pursuit of the trundling, swaying wagon, and leapt to get a handhold on the tailgate. He vaulted himself up and through the canvas flaps as the wagon started the tight turn, splashing into the stream. His anxious eyes raked over the quivering flesh of the two tigers, who hurled themselves at the bars: claws extended and fangs bared. "It is so wonderful you are unharmed," he whispered. Then he crouched in a corner of the wagon, just out of reach of the sharply pointed claws, and took out his harmonica. He began to play.

Jo Jo Lamont screamed and whirled around, dropping the Winchester and covering her mouth with her hands. But the nausea rose despite her efforts to hold it down: the bile erupted by the sight of entrails spilling from burst open flesh as a rear wheel of the wagon sliced through the body of the dead man in the stream.

"For Christsake, Edge!" Case shrieked. Now he was able to move, but only to the extent of raising a foot and stamping it back to the ground.

"Don't like getting shot at, feller!" the half-breed called to him as the swaying wagon came back on a straight course, heading for the brow of the hill at the maximum speed the team was able to haul its heavy burden.

It had been a suicidal attack against a man with a

repeating rifle he knew how to use. But that hadn't been the plan, of course. Grainger, Salter and the bunch of drifters they or Clarence French had gathered must have been watching from the cover of the hill crest as the carny wagons halted at the campsite behind the beach. The presence of Case aboard the cage wagon and Edge riding escort would have told the two former guards which vehicle carried the precious freight. Confirmation would have been provided by how low the wagon rested on its springs. The two ex-guards would have known there would be no trouble from the others. So all that was necessary was to kill the half-breed. Case would not have stood a chance with his pathetically inadequate multi-barrel handgun. Singh had no stomach for fighting. But Grainger had shot the half-breed's horse instead of the man and the attack was in full flood before this fact was realized. The intervention of Jo Jo Lamont? There were variables in every situation. The chances of them happening were higher where women were involved.

"I come to look after my most beautiful beasts, sahib!" the Nepalese shouted, pushing his head out through the front flaps of the wagon as the team achieved the top of the rise and lunged into greater speed going down the other side. "Whatever you feel necessary to do, you do alone. Not for eighty dollars a day will I partake of violence."

Edge had seen Grainger slumped on the hillside, the blood from his shattered head already congealing as the flies fed avidly. Then his narrowed eyes had raked the terrain spread out before him: rolling, brush-covered hills featured with stands of timber. This, soft-looking, strip of country changed suddenly about a mile ahead, where a rocky cliff face reared high, cleaved at one point by the mouth of a ravine.

And he saw the two horsemen on the crest of another hill, galloping hard towards the split in the cliff and already halfway there.

"It's your tigers Case is buying," Edge yelled, hauling on the reins to drive the straining team on a diagonal line down the slope. "And this rig. You're just along for the incidental music. Keep the cat quiet, uh?"

Singh looked fearfully down the slope, towards the sun-sparkled stream which they were approaching at a breakneck pace. The bank on the far side had become an escarpment at the base of a hill. Rock for the most part, which looked terrifyingly capable of smashing the team and the wagon to pieces. The little dark-skinned man screwed his eyes tight shut, then ducked back inside the wagon. Trembling, he squatted in a corner and brought the mouth organ to his lips. Its mournful music was this time designed to calm himself as much as his animals.

The half-breed heard the wailing notes faintly above the thud of pumping hooves, creak of harness and rattling of speeding wheels. Sweat beads stood out against his weathered, deeply-scored face. More salty moisture oozed from every pore in his body, sticking his clothing to his body. He licked wetness from his thin lips and kept his eyes narrowed to mere slips to stop his vision blurring. The timing of the turn had to be precise. If he gave the team free rein, they would veer to the left too soon, with risk of overturning the heavy wagon on the final, steepest section of the slope. And if he left it too late there would not be enough space or time. The horses would make it, but the front corner of the careering wagon would smash into the escarpment.

"*Yoooooowwwweeeeee!*" he yelled, wrenched on the left hand reins, and stomped on the stock of the

Winchester as it started to slide off the footboards.

The lead pair of horses were in the stream, kicking up spray. They responded to the pull of the reins, the sense of urgency witnessed by their own eyes emphasized by the full-throated cry of Edge. The rear pair followed the same line, curving down off the sloping bank to plunge along the water course. Drenching coolness spraying over their lathered flesh drove them back from the brink of a panicked bolt. All four reacted to the skillful handling of the reins, galloping on a course dictated by the driver.

The wagon tilted dangerously as it dipped into the water. As it turned, canvas was ripped to shreds between immoveable rock and the rigid iron bars of the cages dragged along its weather-roughened surface. Then the speeding wagon slammed down on to all four wheels again and began to pitch and roll as the rims bounced over the rock-strewn bed of the stream.

The music from the harmonica became frenetic and tuneless, as the terrified Singh forgot his skill with the instrument and simply blew into it: for no other purpose than to fill his own ears with the discordant sound. Anything was better than the barrage of other noises which he was sure meant the wagon was breaking up as a prelude to his death.

The half-breed allowed himself a short, taut smile of triumph at making the turn with no more damage than a torn side canvas. Then he became cold-eyed and machine-like again, his physical strength concentrating upon retaining control of the team and wagon while his mind worked on the evidence picked up by his eyes, peering ahead from under the hooded lids.

The stream had to come from the base of the cliff, or even along the ravine which cut into the rearing rock face. The water course would have found the easiest route to the ocean. And, provided there were no waterfalls or rapids, it might just point the easiest way inland. In the absence of such obstacles, its meandering course had to be less arduous than the steep rises and sharp falls of the brush-covered hills. Maybe not for a man on a horse, but certainly for a wagon laden with a ton and a half of gold and two angry tigers.

So the half-breed had made the choice and now he peered ahead, looking for white water that would indicate the presence of large, wheel-breaking rocks beneath the surface of the stream. But, at each turn, a further stretch of calm water was revealed, shining in tranquil innocence beneath the fierce light of the sun. And, despite the many curves around the bases of the rises, the stream was leading the way inexorably towards the mouth of the ravine.

The wagon came clear of the broken terrain immediately opposite the gigantic split in the high rock face. A grassy meadow stretched away in either direction from the banks of the stream. When the half-breed had steered the team up out of the water with no slackening of speed, the wheels ran across the springy turf with luxurious smoothness. The water course pointed a sparkling finger into the ravine and Edge held the wagon in that direction, after a glance to right and left had revealed no sign of the two riders.

"It is because of the purity of my life that I have been most fortunately saved yet agin," Singh exclaimed in delight as he interrupted his discordant music to look out through the flap.

"What about the dame in San Francisco?" Edge growled between gritted teeth, easing back on the reins to slacken the headlong pace. There were a lot of niches in the rocky walls of the ravine and scattered boulders on the ground. A hundred and one places two men and their horses could hide.

The Nepalese split his face into a teeth gleaming grin. "A man's most natural urges are not diminished when he leaves his wife half a world away, sahib. God is not a torturer. He would not make man suffer most nasty urge in lower regions. Therefore not impure to scatter fruit of loins when so many passion flowers provided for him."

"Your wife agrees with that?" the half-breed asked as the wagon hurtled into the ravine, deeply shadowed on one side now that the sun had started its afternoon descent.

"Wife never close by when matter arises, sahib."

"Guess she wouldn't be," Edge muttered, leaning to one side and glancing to the rear of the wagon for the first time since the careering pursuit had begun. But there was nothing to see except the brush-covered hills and isolated clumps of trees, with the ocean a thin blue line on the far horizon. For, as the ravine swung to the right, the second wagon to leave the trail was screened by the high angle of towering rock.

"Oh, goodness gracious me!" Singh cried, the old terror re-emerging to swamp the good humor in his tone.

Edge swung his attention to the front again. Two loose horses, still saddled, lifted their heads from chomping a patch of tough grass, and bolted out of the path of the wagon. He saw wood splinter from the seat six inches from his leg before he heard the sharp crack of the rifle's report.

"It is indeed a day of much shooting I am thinking!" Singh yelled, and ducked back through the flap, pitching full length to the bed of the wagon and covering his head with his hands. The tigers roared. "Shut up, you bloody ugly brutes!" he screamed at them.

The brake blocks screeched against the wheel rims as Edge hauled on the lever. His free hand wrenched back on the reins, jerking up the heads of the team. The wagon side-slid around the curve of the ravine, spilling a great billow of dust behind it. Fighting to bring the snorting, sweating horses to a halt, the half-breed caught just a glimpse of the two men. The ravine was a dead end and they were crouched on a ledge a hundred feet up the rock wall. Nature, or the men themselves, had heaped loose rocks into a barricade on the lip of the ledge and it was over this dry-stone wall that they were firing.

A whole fusillade of bullets was sent crashing down towards the wagon before the team finally came to a panting, snorting halt. Edge was already crouched low on the seat as the lead whined about him, smashing more splinters of wood and boring holes in the canvas. The moment the wagon jerked to a halt, he powered into a leap to the ground, scooping up the rifle as he came clear. He hit the dirt sure-footed, turned and dived between the front and rear wheels. Dirt spurted from under his heels as bullets dug into the ground. Beneath the wagon, the settling dust clinging to his sweat-tacky face, Edge was in secure cover and the rifle fire stopped. His long, brown fingers extracted shells from the left side of his gunbelt and he pushed them through the Winchester's loading gate, replacing those fired back at the camp by the beach.

"Hey, you down there!" one of the men on the ledge yelled, and laughter ripped from his mouth in a short burst. "Reckon you driven yourself into a trap."

The tigers had been roaring, but with the end of the gunfire, they had become quiet again, except for an occasional low growl.

"Oh, dear dear me," the Nepalese moaned. "Do you think he is right, sahib?"

Singh had his eye close to a crack between two boards in the wagon bed and was peering down at Edge. The half-breed looked up at the single dark eye between the boards and sighed.

"Sometimes I don't think you've got a hell of a lot of faith in me, feller," he muttered, pushing the final shell into the gate. He worked the lever to eject a spent casing and thrust a live bullet into the breach.

"I am ever ready to be convinced, sahib," the Nepalese answered hurriedly.

"You hear me down there?"

Edge spat, arching the globule out of the shade beneath the wagon into the sun-bleached dust.

"He hears you, Harv," the second man on the ledge yelled, and giggled. "Seems to make him spittin' mad."

"Look at it this way," Edge said softly, a pensive expression on his hard-skinned, lean features. "Didn't have a snowball's chance in hell of catching up with them unless they wanted to be caught up with. And, bearing in mind what this rig is carrying, beside big cats, I figured they'd want to get caught up with."

"You are indeed one smart sahib," Singh allowed after a tense pause. "But I think bullets can hurt you just the same as stupid Nepalese like Viswabandhu Nageshwar Singh. And not only hurt, you understand."

"Hey, we got us enough ammo to stand off an army!" Harv warned. "You just back off and leave the wagon, we won't shoot."

Edge inched forward, between the front wheels, and peered up at the rock face between the hindquarters of the two rear horses. He could see rifle barrels poking out over the barricade of stones. But both men

91

stayed in solid cover. He moved to one side and then the other, surverying the floor of the ravine and the surface of the cliff below, to right and left and above the ledge. There were a dozen ways to get up to and above where the men were positioned. But not without a worse than fifty-fifty chance of taking at least one bullet before the closest group of covering boulders was reached. But, if the two men up there chose the right route, they could make it to ground level without showing a hat brim or boot heel.

"I decide to put faith in you, sahib," Singh said. "Because there is nothing else for it. Oh, dear, dear me, no."

"Obliged," Edge said wryly, then raised his voice as he inched backwards, towards the rear of the wagon. "You up there!"

"He's ready to talk turkey, Harv."

"And I figured he was a chicken."

"What cut of the gold French giving you?" the half-breed yelled.

"Who the hell's French? Ray Grainger and his buddy hired me and my brother and the other guys outta Yellowtown. Even divvy all round." He laughed. "Seems me and Jesse get to have a half share each. Cause we ain't makin' no deals, mister."

Edge lowered the Winchester over the tailgate, then hooked his hands over the wood and hauled himself up and through the flap. Singh was crouching in a corner at the front, looking very frightened. The stench of animal excrement was almost overpowering under the canvas. From the ledge, there was no way to see inside through the large rent in the side canvas.

"Yellowtown next place we supposed to give show," the Nepalese imparted, just for something to say.

The tigers were lying each side of the block of gold: content until they picked up the scent of the intruder. Then they bared their yellow fangs and growled with soft menace, evil hatred emanating from their blazing eyes.

"How well trained are the cats?" Edge asked softly.

"You gonna back off?" Harv demanded, impatience giving his voice a tone of anger.

Despite the situation, Singh could smile with genunine pride. "They best trained animals in the whole world, sahib. I wrestle with them. Put my head in their mouths. They eat from amy hand. Rear on hind legs. These fine, well-trained tigers, I am telling you. They do most things excepting only talk."

Edge grimaced at the gleaming eyes and the vicious teeth revealed by the curled back lips. "Always been a dog man myself," he muttered. "How'd it be if we turned them loose?"

"Oh, goodness gracious, sahib!" Singh exclaimed.

"No way you can get that wagon outta this hole in the ground!" Harv yelled. "What the hell's the use of waitin' around in the hot sun for?"

"You must understand, sahib. They are wild beasts. For most of time, I am their master. They obey me like my many children in Nepal. But wild beasts. For you cannot always trust them. Oh, dear, dear me, no. And they have had much annoyance the last night and today. I would not like to trust them. I could not be responsible for the actions of the beasts."

"No sweat, feller," Edge said. "I'll take any complaints."

The door of the cage was secured by a metal pin dropped through four brackets. It made a piercing screech coming clear. Singh gasped, but the warning stuck in his throat. The tigers pricked their ears and cocked their heads to one side at the sound. Edge dropped the securing pin to the wagon bed and eased open the door with the Winchester barrel. As it swung wide, he stepped to the side of the cage, into the nine inches of space between the bars and the sideboard of the wagon. He kept the rifle aimed at the nearest tiger, in case the big cat decided to try a mauling claw through the bars. The sweat of heat and tension trickled down his back: and seemed to turn to ice when the tiger rose lazily up on to its feet. He completely ignored the man, looking at the open doorway with detached interest. Then he yawned and padded forward. He halted on the threshold of the cage, ears pricked and eyes wide to stare out through the flap at the rear of the wagon. The other tiger joined him, decided to throw caution to the wind, and leapt in a powerful spring: clearing the tailgate and brushing the canvas aside. The second animal gave a low growl of agreement with the move and imitated the jump to freedom.

"God Almighty, Harv!" Jesse shrieked. "The bastard's turned the cats loose."

"Blast 'em!" Harv snarled.

"My tigers!" Singh screamed, and lunged towards the rear of the wagon.

On the opposite side of the cage, Edge went forward, knocking aside the front flaps of canvas with the Winchester barrel as a fusillade of shots exploded from the ledge. He could see the two men, raised up behind their barricade to aim down into the ravine. He fired and saw the man on the right fall backwards out of sight. The man's rifle clattered against the rocky barricade. The splash of blood made less sound.

"I'm hit, Harv!" Jesse yelled in alarm. "God Almighty, I'm hit."

The injured man's brother stopped firing and ducked out of sight before the half-breed could swing the Winchester to the second target. Singh was crouched at the tailgate, peering anxiously through the flap.

94

Edge crouched over him to look out at the cats. They were prowling casually towards the spot where the source of the stream sprang from the base of one of the ravine's walls. Their heads moved from side to side, eyes alert to catch dangerous movement. But there was a certain arrogant nonchalance in the animals' gait.

"They don't look so wild to me," the half-breed muttered.

His voice was low, but the tigers heard it. They stopped in their tracks and turned their heads to look menacingly back at the wagon. They growled.

"Please, sahib, I must request you to be most quiet indeed," the little Nepalese urged, his voice barely audible. "There is no telling what tigers will do."

One of the animals padded forward again, and stretched his head out towards the clear water bubbling from the rock face. But the other remained immobile, except for a twitching of his nostrils.

"He has scent he knows," Singh said. "Perhaps he knows it wrong to be free. Will come back into cage if I order."

"Don't reckon it's curry sweat he smells, feller," Edge replied, lowering his voice to the same level as Singh. "Guess he knows what fresh blood smells like, uh?"

The tiger gave another low growl, and saliva slavered from his gaping mouth. The second cat finished drinking, raised his head, and caught the same scent of Jesse's spilled blood. Both animals stared beyond the wagon and up at the rocky wall of the ravine's dead end.

"Oh dear, dear me!" Singh murmured, shaking his head. "You have shot one of men?"

"Reckon so," Edge replied. "Less he carries a bottle of ketchup around with him."

95

"Oh, goodness gracious me. Indeed, my beautiful tigers have scented raw meat. They will be shot."

The striped cats were on the move again, staying in the shade at the base of the ravine wall. The heat, or caution, kept their pace slow. Padding along, sniffing the air and dripping saliva, they were easy targets.

"No way to speed them up?" Edge asked, his voice a harsh whisper as the tigers drew level with the rear of the wagon, and sent a pair of sneering looks towards it.

"Perhaps there is, my goodness gracious," Singh said tensely, and drew the mouth organ from his pocket. "I hate British Raj in India, sahib. Oh, most certainly so. Teach my beautiful tigers to hate, too. Especially do we despise the Queen Victoria, whom I ask God most certainly not to bless. My tigers, they are trained not to like British National Anthem, sahib. I play this song, and tigers they get very angry, oh dear, dear me, yes."

"So play it," Edge encouraged.

"But there is danger they turn to attack us, sahib." Singh's dark-skinned face was a mask of awesome foreboding.

Edge caressed the stock of the Winchester. "We got nothing to lose except a couple of tigers, feller. And they're going to be steaks and spare ribs anyway if they don't quit strolling."

Singh gave a shrug of resignation and raised the harmonica to his mouth. "If necessary to kill, you do it quick, please? Not wish my magnificent beasts to suffer."

The half-breed eyed the slavering jaws of the prowling tigers. "No sweat, feller," he promised. "They won't even get the time to have their teeth on Edge."

He aimed the rifle as the anxious Singh took a deep breath and expelled it through the mouth organ. The incongruous strains of *God Save The Queen* floated through the hot air trapped between the walls of the rocky ravine. Nobody stood to attention. The Nepalese leaned against the barred doorway of the cage. Edge inserted his head and the Winchester barrel through the rear flap. Harv peered over the barricade, concern for his brother, fear of the tigers and bewilderment at the strange music constantly rearranging the lines of his stubbled face. The two big cats halted for an instant, jaws gaping wide and flanks quivering. Both looked towards the wagon from where the music came, then snapped their heads around, eyes blazing in the direction from which their twitching nostrils picked up the scent of fresh blood. Then, with twin roars, they agreed to combine an outlet for their rage with the almost as powerful need to satisfy their hunger.

They lunged towards the rock face blocking off the ravine.

"Play it again, Singh!" Edge rasped, swinging around and squeezing hurriedly through the narrow gap to get to the front of wagon.

"Jesus!" Harv yelled, and a shot rang out.

Edge burst his head and shoulders through the front flap, slamming the rifle barrel across the top of the seat back rest. Harv fired again. But he had lost all interest in the wagon. He was standing erect, Winchester stock tight against his shoulder as he blasted towards the base of cliff. The tigers, incensed into greater anger by the crack of gunfire against the plaintive notes of the hated music, leapt agilely from rock to rock, foothold to foothold.

"You get 'em?" Jesse yelled, his voice high-pitched by terror. "God Almighty, my arm! You get 'em cats, Harv?"

"Shut your friggin' mouth!" Harv bellowed.

Edge could have killed him, with a heart or a head

shot. Instead, he took careful aim on the man's right hip as Harv tried frantically to draw a bead on the leaping tigers. Red blossomed on Harv's pants just above the butt of the sixgun jutting from his holster. He screamed and was powered back against the cliff face. The rifle fell from his hands and he twisted into a crumple behind the barricade.

"Oh, you sonofabitching bastard!" he shrieked.

Singh had leapt down from the rear of the wagon without faltering in his playing. Now, as he watched his tigers climb lithely closer to their quarry, his dark eyes widened with excitement. Edge watched the cats, too, coldly enjoying their natural cunning as they leapt from one piece of cover to the next. They stayed wide of the ledge until they were above it. Then they angled back. One of the brothers on the ledge saw a flash of yellow and black striping. A revolver cracked and rock splinters erupted close to the animal.

Singh stopped playing and the silence in the ravine was complete, save for a low, almost pleasant-to-listen-to growling from each tiger. Then, systematically, his eyes narrowed to glinting slits and his mouth set in a thin line, the half-breed emptied the Winchester towards the rock face. He raked the barrel to left and right a few degrees, sending a spray of lead skimming across the top of the barricade. The brothers yelled in alarm as fragments of blasted rocks rained down on them.

"Are my beautiful beasts not magnificent?" Singh cried, jumping up and down as the two tigers crouched above the ledge.

The Winchester's firing pin stabbed into an empty breech. The tigers growled, the sound of their anger and hunger resounding between the walls of the ravine. Harv and Jesse screamed. The tigers plunged downwards—claws extended and fangs dripping with saliva. A rifle and a revolver exploded. The bullets whined past the leaping forms to streak high towards the cobalt blueness of the sky.

"Reckon I'll stay a dog man," the half-breed muttered, continuing to watch the ledge as he climbed out through the flap, then leapt down from the wagon seat.

The rocks which had formed the barricade began to topple and rain down the cliff face. But the sound of their descent was swamped by the awesome venting of animal rage and human agony. As the barricade crumbled, Edge and Singh were able to see more than just the leaping, quivering forms of the tigers. They saw the two men wrestling with the ravenous cats, fixing and then losing ineffectual hand-holds on the striped coats. Their shirts were already slick with flowing blood. Too much to have spurted from bullet wounds.

"You figure you can get them back in cage, feller?" Edge asked, moving towards the foot of the cliff.

"My tigers always most amenable after eating, sahib," Singh replied. "Oh dear, dear me, yes. I always feed them before show."

One of the men screamed to the point where his voice broke. Something less solid than rock dropped from the ledge and thudded to the ground beside Edge. He looked down coldly at a bitten off arm, oozing blood from the teeth-marked elbow. A Remington revolver was clutched in the hand. Along the barrel was some scratched lettering: Harvey P. Hill.

"Fussy eaters," he muttered, and glanced upwards. A tiger, jaws dripping blood, stared down at him, then disappeared. There were no more screams and the tigers had moderated their roars to low growls. The struggle was over. The kills had been made. The wet sounds of tearing flesh and the crunch of teeth

99

on bone had lost the quality of urgency. The tigers were feeding.

Edge went up at one side of the cliff, empty Winchester crooked under an arm and his right hand draped over the butt of the holstered Colt. The Nepalese took another route, making soothing music with the harmonica. He was the first to reach a point level with the ledge, for he went closer to where the big cats were feeding. Pride, rather than horror, showed in his eyes at the sight which greeted him. The half-breed climbed higher, and looked down on the ledge from far to the right. His lean features were set in an impassive expression. Harv and Jesse had twice tried to kill him and they had paid the price of failure. The manner of their deaths was unimportant, so long as they died.

Their faces had been clawed to ribbons of crimson flesh. Their bodies and limbs had been torn to pieces. Great bites had been taken out of their chests and stomach, and gory entrails and organs were spread across the ledge. One of the brothers had lost both arms at the shoulder. The other still had an arm, but both his legs had been chewed through to the gleaming bone. Even as Edge and Singh watched, one of the tigers held a body still while he ripped at a leg calf with his fangs. The chunk of meat was torn free and the tiger ate it with relish. Flies swarmed up from old wounds to settle upon the new one.

The two men watched, the half-breed silently and the Nepalese playing soft music, as two more were eaten: until the tigers were satiated with warm, raw meat. Then both animals belched, licked the blood from their lips and stood up, stretching their powerful bodies and limbs in contentment.

Singh lowered the harmonica and sighed. "I cannot

be responsible that wild animals are not non-violent, sahib," he called.

Edge spat. "Reckon they got what it takes to do things their own way."

The tigers purred, undisturbed by the voices of the men.

"They very amenable now, Sahib," Singh announced with high confidence. "Do things my way. Go back into cage and sleep or perform in show."

"Seen them acting up enough for one day," Edge replied evenly, looking down at the clawed heads, mutilated torsoes and scattering of bones which were all that remained of Harv and Jesse Hill.

"They did very well indeed, I think, sahib." The Nepalese nodded his head rapidly. "You see how they attack when I play anthem of Queen Victoria, who I ask God most certainly not to bless? As hated British say, most jolly good show."

"I saw it," the half-breed answered. "The Hills died with the sound of music."

CHAPTER SEVEN

Edge wiped the sweat from his forehead with the back of a hand and then rasped his fingers over the stubble on his jaw. He was still perched on the rock from which he had watched the tigers finishing their meal of human flesh. Singh was down on the ledge now, muttering softly in his native tongue to the animals. The tigers squatted on their haunches, watching their trainer sleepily. The Nepalese trod softly and moved his skinny body smoothly. Not until he had taken a position between the two animals and was stroking the fur at their necks did the half-breed move his hand away from the butt of the revolver. Singh looked up at him and grinned.

"Is this not a more wonderful sight than a block of gold, sahib?"

"Real wild," the half-breed replied, and dug into his shirt pocket for the makings as he swung his head to glance down into the ravine.

"Git up there!" Walter Peat yelled, and cracked the reins across the backs of the team.

Arabella was up on the seat of the cage wagon beside him. She was aiming a rifle and Edge powered off the rock. His hip cracked painfully against the stock of the Winchester as he smacked into the sharply sloping ground. He cursed as he recalled he had not reloaded the rifle. The girl's weapon exploded and rock fragments showered from the cliff face above him. The tigers growled. Edge saw the suddenly terrified Singh as the Nepalese jerked his hands away from the animals' necks.

The half-breed snatched the Colt from his holster. But Singh's predicament did not concern him. He bellied forward, around the rock on which he had been perched, and peered down at the floor of the ravine. The mouth organ began to issue mournful music. The tigers purred. Walter Peat was lashing and yelling the team into a tight turn. The Colt bucked in Edge's hand, but the range was too long for accuracy with a sixgun. Dirt spurted through the dust raised by pumping hooves and spinning wheels.

The couple's wagon was parked at the angle of rock where the ravine turned towards its dead end. Seeing it, the two horse team standing contentedly in the shade, Edge realized Peat and the girl must have driven up while he and Singh were climbing the rock face. The struggle of men and animals on the ledge had held their attention: and the roars and the screams had covered all other sounds.

Now, as Edge holstered the Colt and fed a shell into the Winchester's loading gate, it was the raucous noise of the hurtling wagon that filled the ravine. Two more rifle shots cracked as he slammed the stock against his shoulder. The contented horses in the traces of the parked wagon died on their feet. Both collapsed to the side, gushing blood from the expertly placed wounds between their eyes. The half-breed's single shot ricochetted off a front wheel rim and spun over the backs of the rear pair hauling the cage wagon. Then the team and the wagon were out of sight, protected by the solid cover of the rock wall. The sound of their hurtling progress diminished.

Edge began to reload the rifle and Singh stopped playing the harmonica. He turned to look sadly up at Edge as he stroked the neck fur of the purring tigers.

"Oh dear, dear me, sahib," the little Nepalese called, shaking his head. "What a calamity it is. The fire eater and the dancing lady are indeed most wicked people."

"Don't deserve to live," the half-breed answered, continuing to feed shells through the loading gate of the Winchester.

Singh became anxious. "My tigers, they are no longer hungry, sahib."

"They did a good job," Edge told him. "You reckon you can get them back to the beach?"

"My beautiful beasts most amenable. If there is rope in wagon of fire eater, be no trouble. If no rope, only a little trouble. What I tell Case? He most certainly be most angry to hear his big gold stolen."

The half-breed finished loading the rifle and showed Singh a cold grin. "If he bad mouths you, set the cats on to him. Then tell him to expect me in Yellowtown, gold and all."

"He bound to ask when, sahib?"

Edge was already starting down the rock face, more conscious of the tigers' curious stares than the anxious look in their trainer's eyes. He took great care not to get directly beneath the ledge where the cats were perched, flanking Singh.

"Carny's got a fortune teller."

"I wish you great good luck, sahib," the Nepalese called after him. "Eight dollar a day is more than I earn with my beautiful tigers."

"And it doesn't cost you anything for feed," Edge muttered as he reached the floor of the ravine and broke into a run.

The tracks were easy to follow at first through the loose dust of the ravine and then east over the turf to the meadowland at the foot of the cliff. The half-breed never ran at the limit of his capabilities, and at intervals slowed from the loping gait to a fast walk. He had no canteen, but the hill country abounded with streams. He paused at each one, to replenish his body with moisture which the blazing afternoon sun sweated out of him.

He was heading inland, but the blue line of the ocean was always in sight when he glanced over his shoulder. For the terrain rose steadily towards the peaks of the Cascade Mountains. When the strip of grassland petered out, the ground became hard-packed dirt and rock. But, because of the heavy freight it carried, the wagon was never able to travel very far without leaving some sign of its passage, be it the hoofbeat of a straining horse or the narrow rut engraved by a turning wheel. The weight and the almost constant upgrade kept its speed low. But the terrain, combined with the heat, also slowed the half-breed. And lack of food made itself felt after the advance of the evening had extracted the fierceness from the reddening sun.

There was game in the mountain foothills, but he didn't try to shoot any. Firstly he was reluctant to use time in lighting a fire and cooking the meat. Secondly, a shot could well alert the gold stealers. Although he was on foot, he knew there was a good chance he had closed up on his quarry. He was hungry, but he had been fresh at the start of the chase. The team had hauled the heavy wagon along the trail all morning, then been forced to gallop at full stretch across rugged country. They had to be rested at intervals, and for longer periods than it took Edge to suck up water from the streams he had used.

The terrain was much more rugged now, as a brightly moonlit night closed in on the mountains. Rock faces rose all around and the isolated stands of redwoods had been replaced by extensive swathes of firs. The wagon could be rolling or halted, beyond every rise or turn that Edge made. And if Walter Peat and Arabella were unaware they were being followed, he didn't want to alert them.

He saw them when the night had advanced far enough for every vestige of the day's heat to have been sucked away. At a time when the sweat holding his clothes to his body had dried and become cold. And when he was having wishful thoughts about the fur-lined coat strapped to his bedroll on the dead stallion. He picked his way through a scattering of boulders in the deep moon shadow of a grotesquely shaped rocky outcrop and saw he had been right not to follow the sign the long way around. For he emerged at the top of a sharp drop surfaced with loose shale. Spread out from the base was a broad area of dusty flatness. The moonlight showed clearly the tracks of the wagon and team, curving across this area from the far side of the outcrop to the cluster of buildings huddled on the bank of a stream where the ground began to rise again.

The town, if the dozen or so buildings could be called such, was laid out around a square. A few shacks dotted the far slope, each beside the mouth of a tunnel driven into the hillside. The rusted rails of a narrow gauge track, broken in many places and

106

twisted in others, linked each abandoned mine working and ran down into the town. It, too, had apparently been deserted by its citizens. For, as the half-breed raked his hooded eyes over the scene, across a distance of a thousand feet or so, he saw the larger buildings were as dilapidated as the shacks on the slope above. The moon found few panes of glass to shine on. Porches sagged, doors hung open and roofs were holed. Spring and summer winds had drifted dust into great piles against timber walls and the detrius of rocks and tree branches from the winter-flooded stream scattered across the central square. The wagon was parked close in to the side of a building at the entry to the square. The team was ground hobbled on a patch of grass at the bank of the stream. The flickering red of firelight rather than the steady glow of yellow lamplight was a square beacon at one glassless window. There was no sound except for the rippling of the slow running stream which curled around the rise, swung across in front of the town and then continued on a northern course.

Edge worked the lever action of the Winchester and the metallic scraping seemed to resound between the shale covered slope and the less steep gradient behind the town. But the horses on the bank of the stream did not even prick their ears. No shadows moved across the firelit window. He tested the shale, setting down a booted foot lightly. Fragments of rock spilled away from beneath his heel. To his own ears the noise of tumbling stones sounded like a full-scale avalanche shattering the peace surrounding the derelict town. He withdrew his foot hurriedly and crouched down, pushing the Winchester into the dust and covering his gunbelt with his arms. When a man moved to the window to stare out, the form of Edge was just another shadow among the boulders at the top of the shale slope. Neither guns nor shells reflected a tell-tale glint of moonlight.

Edge heard words, too distant to be distinct. A short exchange of conversation. All he could be sure of was that two men had spoken to each other. There had definitely not been a woman's voice. The man retreated into the room from the window, and Edge rose and backed off from the top of the slope. Recalling what Harvey Hill had said in response to his question about Clarence French, the half-breed wondered if he had tied the fat man in with the wrong gold-stealers. The buggy and the white gelding could well be down there at the abandoned town, hidden to him by the group of buildings.

Because of the risks presented by the loose shale, he had to follow the tracks of the wagon which swung wide of the outcrop at the top of the rise. This added almost thirty minutes to the final leg of the pursuit, but he didn't hurry. Peat, or whoever else had come to the window, had seemed to be convinced an animal or bird had disturbed the shale. Edge wanted the gold stealers to settle down completely before running the risk of attracting their attention again.

Beyond the rock pinnacle, he emerged on to an overgrown trail, as disused as the mineworkings and the town. When he saw it, a tight grin folded back his lips, for it twisted through the rugged terrain in a south-western direction. If Yellowtown was the only community of any size in the area, there was a good chance the trail led down to there from the mountains. The slope down into the dish of land cradling the ghost town, now host to the living, was at this point firm with hard-packed earth. But he didn't start to descend yet. It was too open, and bathed with pale moonlight. Anything moving against the sun bleached ground would be clearly visible from below. So he moved around on the rim of the bowl, careful not to skyline himself in the gaps between the peaks and ridges of higher ground. He did not start to go downwards until he was behind the town, on the rise pitted with mine tunnels. From the cover of one of the shacks, which had been weathered to no more than four walls surrounding the collapsed roof, he looked at the town from a new vantage point. He saw there was no buggy or white horse down there. A sign above the doorway of the broken down shack caught his narrowed eyes. The faded lettering was just discernible: SILVER CITY NO. 6 SHAFT.

Because of the way in which the tunnels had been driven into the hillside, each with its adjacent shack, he took a zigzagging route down to the town. He reached level ground beside a bank of earth surrounded by timber at the end of the narrow gauge railroad track. There was a long platform here, with another faded sign: SILVER CITY DEPOT. Two rusted iron trucks were canted on their sides, leaning against the platform. Rusted picks, spades and pails had spilled from the trucks and lay scattered around. He moved around the platform to avoid treading on the rotted timbers and went between a two and a one story building. The horses whinnied and pricked their ears. Then they quietened. His footfalls were silent on the accumulated dust of neglect. The larger building—the only two story one in Silver City—was a saloon and hotel. On the other side of the gap was a livery stable. Stores, an assay office, a warehouse, a blacksmith's forge and a church with a collapsed steeple comprised the remainder of Silver City. Walter Peat, Arabella and at least one other man were in the assay office. The acrid smell of their fire could not quite mask the dank odor

109

of rotted timber that emanated from every other building.

Smoke from the chimney and a strip of red light at the foot of the door told Edge where his quarry were located, over at the north west corner of the square. He was on the east side. There was adequate cover from boulders and tree stumps to invite him into an approach across the square. But the buildings offered more secure protection.

"Drop the rifle!"

He recognized the voice of Arabella, rasping out the words from behind him just as he started to swing around. He froze, half-turned. The Winchester was held low down on his left side. His right hand was at his jaw, the fingers having just run over the twenty-four hour growth of stubble. There was a chance that, as he released the rifle, he could turn, draw the Colt and fire. But maybe it wasn't necessary to take chances. The girl had spoken to him instead of blasting a bullet into his back. He let the Winchester fall into the dust. His hands maintained their positions.

"Now unbuckle the gunbelt." Her voice sounded less dangerously nervous. "Use your left hand."

He had her exactly placed now. Behind him and to the left. She must have been waiting, her breath held inside the bursting lungs, beyond the doorless doorway of the saloon's side entrance. It was awkward, working with his weaker hand on the belt-buckle. It took a long time to get the leather free of the clasp. Perhaps a full minute. The girl breathed hard all the while. Then she gave a sigh of relief as the long, brown fingers loosened the cord at the inside of the thigh and the belt and holster thudded into the dust.

"You do his shooting and his guarding for him," Edge said softly. "I guess he washes the dishes, uh?"

"Walk out into the square," Arabella instructed.

110

"Towards the doorway with the light showing at the bottom."

"What if I don't?"

"Then I'll shoot you."

Edge turned his head slowly, to look over his shoulder. She was standing precisely where he had visualized her, framed in the doorway. A long, thick coat was worn, cape-fashion, over her shoulders, reaching three-quarters of the way down her flared dress. Her face was very pale against the dark coloring of her hair. Fear lit her eyes.

"I think I believe you, ma'am," he said.

"You'd better." The Winchester jerked, beckoning him to move forward. But the muzzle never wavered wide of the target.

"Saw me coming, uh?" Edge asked, turning his head to face forward and starting to go in the direction she had ordered.

"Walt thought it was a rabbit made those stones start to roll," she answered. Eagerly, as though she welcomed the chance to talk—to calm her nerves. "He always takes things for granted."

The half-breed spat. "Reckon he took the gold for profit."

"He didn't think you'd follow us. But he had too much on his mind in the Seascape saloon to be watching you very closely, Mr. Edge. I watched you. And I saw what kind of man you were."

"What kind's that, ma'am." He picked his way through the debris of old floods. They were out of the shadows of the buildings now, the silvered moonlight stretching their own shadows long across the littered square.

"The hard kind. The kind that doesn't quit easy. I kept telling him that when he reckoned it was easy to get the gold after it only had but the one guard."

"Turned out he was right there, though."

"Sure. So when I told him that keeping it was going to be tough, he wasn't about to listen to me."

"Should have blasted me back at the ravine, ma'am."

"That's what Walt wanted me to do. But I ain't never killed anybody before. You don't just turn into a murderer at the drop of a hat."

"Not even with a solid gold reason?"

"Stop right there!" she said, her voice hardening. "And don't get any ideas. I tried to hit you in the leg at the ravine. From this range, I can't miss."

They were halfway across the square.

"Haven't got an idea in my head," Edge told her as he halted, and watched her shadow.

She closed in on him, narrowing the gap from six feet to three: between his back and the muzzle of the rifle. "Walt!" she yelled. "I told you Walt. Look what I found!"

"Watched me all the way down, uh?" the half-breed asked evenly.

"From the crest of the rise where you crossed the old trail," she replied.

The windows of the assay office were covered with black paint, and squares of boarding where the panes were broken. The door opened fast and a shaft of firelight fell into the square. Then Peat's shadow interrupted it. For a moment, as he stared out into the lower light level, he showed fear. But then, as he saw Arabella holding the Winchester on the tall half-breed, a broad grin spread across his youth face. He was holding a short-length, brass-barrelled blunderbuss. Emerging from the office he had been tense and ready to point the gun in any direction. Now he relaxed, and let the muzzle sag to aim at the ground.

"Stay inside, old man," he tossed over his shoulder,

and advanced down from the sidewalk that fronted the buildings along that section of the square.

"I told you that was no rabbit!" Arabella said with a note of scorn in her voice.

"Who is it?"

Approaching the half-breed, he slowed his pace and brought up the stumpy-looking gun to cover him.

"Edge."

"Expecting somebody else?" the half-breed asked evenly, appearing to look towards the advancing fire-eater. But his narrowed eyes were gazing to the left, capturing every movement made by the girl: each of them communicated via her shadow.

"What about the Nep and his cats?" Peat asked.

The query triggered the action which Edge had been poised and waiting for. The even-voiced reminder that two man-eating tigers were loose somewhere in the territory suddenly resurrected fear in the girl. He heard her catch her breath, and saw the flitting of her shadow as she turned to rake terror-filled eyes over the shadowed facades of the buildings and the rising ground beyond.

"Watch it!" Peat screamed. And Edge knew he had called it right. The young fire-eater was less than eight feet in front of him, with the blunderbuss leveled and primed to explode. But Peat didn't only want the gold. He wanted the girl as well. So he wasn't prepared to send a scattering charge of shot towards Edge while Arabella was positioned to get ripped apart by the fringe of the spray.

Edge whirled, folding at the knees and thrusting his arms out to their fullest extent in front of him. He turned in the same direction as the girl. And was facing her as Peat's warning powered her into bringing the gun to bear again. The half-breed ignored the rifle. As his feet pivoted, he raised up on to his toes and lunged at the girl. He went under the arc of the rifle as it swung towards him, his left arm curling around her waist. As he half straightened, the barrel was slanted up towards the night sky.

"Throw the gun!" Peat screamed.

Edge's right hand streaked to the nape of his neck. A shriek of terror and pain ripped from Arabella's lips. Anguish augmented her strength. As the half-breed took a long, swinging stride to step behind her, crushing her sideways on to him, she threw the rifle. Her left hand unfolded from around the mechanism and her right cupped under the base of the stock. She pushed upwards and the Winchester sailed through the air like a misshapen spear.

Peat tried to grab it before it hit the ground, but he missed. He stooped to pick it up, still holding the blunderbuss. The girl's shriek became a sob as the crushing grip around her waist was relaxed. But only for a moment. As she tried to lunge free of Edge's encircling arm, he stepped behind her and tightened his hold again. His hand jerked away from the back of his neck. Moonlight glinted on the blade of the open razor. She felt its cold metal against her cheek, the point resting just under her right eye. Peat straightened up, a weapon held uselessly in each hand. And the futility of being so heavily armed was emphasized when he saw the girl's utter helplessness. Edge tilted the blade so that it no longer lay flat to the soft flesh of the girl. A tiny droplet of blood oozed from a small puncture of the skin.

"Walt!" she gasped.

Peat was too shocked to speak or move for long moments. In that time the bead of blood had spent itself leaving a crimson trail down to Arabella's chin. Then he dropped the ancient blunderbuss and took a two-handed grip on the repeater.

114

"You kill her, you're dead!" He sounded very young and very scared. Which was the way he looked. The girl trembled, but not so much as the boy. The Winchester was canted up from the hip. If he had squeezed the trigger the bullet may or may not have bored into the half-breed's bronzed face visible above Arabella's wan one.

Edge's eyes were slitted. His teeth glinted the brighter when he curled back his lips. The words hissed. "So you got two lives in your hands, feller. Less chance of losing the one you care about if you keep your hands free."

"Please, Walt!" the girl begged. "Drop the gun."

Peat shook his head. "No, honey. He won't hurt you while I've got it."

"Tell him he's making a mistake, ma'am," Edge said softly to Arabella.

"He will, Walt!" she pleaded. "He'll cut me, for sure."

Edge's hand was fisted around the handle of the razor. The rifle wavered in Peat's trembling grasp. Edge turned his wrist. A half inch of the finely honed blade sank into the girl's cheek. It scraped the underside of the bone and pricked her gum. Warm blood spurted over his hand. She screamed.

"Oh, my dear God!" Peat gasped.

The half-breed widened his eyes so that the youngster was certain to see the cold intent visible in them. "Drop the rifle and back off, feller," he ordered softly. "Or start blasting. The suspense is killing her."

Arabella was shaking with sobs and shock. "Do it, Walter!" she screamed at the top of her shrill voice. "Jesus, I'll be scarred for life."

It was as if the Winchester had suddenly become red hot. Peat tore his gaze away from the trap of Edge's stare, looked in horror for an instant at the

115

blade dug into the girl's cheek, then glanced at the rifle. He slammed it down into the dust. He backed away fast, toppling over a tree stump. He picked himself up and widened the gap even further between himself and the guns.

"Let's take a walk, ma'am," Edge muttered, nudging Arabella forward with his body.

She moved, gingerly, the razor blade still inserted through her cheek and pricking at her gums. Peat watched in silent, horrified fascination. Drops of blood ran off Edge's fisted hand and splashed to the dust, spotting the shuffling progress of the couple. When the half-breed was standing between the rifle and the scattergun, he released his grip around the girl's waist. She remained absolutely still. Edge dug his right heel into the ground and raised his toe as he swung it. The Winchester was trapped beneath his foot. Then he powered down into a crouch. His right hand held the razor rigid. The blade remained sunken to a depth of half an inch in her flesh. Its honed edge sliced her face from just beneath the eye until it bounced off her jawbone and came free. Agony and shock froze the scream in her throat, then plunged her into unconsciousness. As the strength went out of her legs, they folded under her and she crumpled into a heap where she had stood.

Edge allowed the crimson-stained razor to slip from his grasp and snatched up the blunderbuss. Peat made to lunge towards the inert Arabella. But the gaping muzzle of the scattergun froze him in an awkward, forward leaning stance.

"Why?" he croaked.

The half-breed sighed. "She heard about my aversion to guns being pointed to me. Did it twice. Once, she even fired at me."

"But she's only a kid," Peat wailed.

116

"Eighteen or nineteen, I'd guess. Ain't exceptionally young by my rules."

"She needs help."

"Not your worry, feller."

"But she is!" he wailed, his voice quivering with anguish. "We're going to be married."

The half-breed shook his head. "You've got a prior engagement."

He squeezed the trigger. The blunderbuss was loaded with a charge of buckshot. Released from their paper wrapper, the pellets roared from the wide bore muzzle through a dense billow of acrid black smoke. They peppered Peat's body from mid-thigh to throat, ripping through his clothes and tearing into his flesh. The impact of the blast lifted him off his feet and hurled him backwards. His dark clothing became sheened with brilliant crimson. He hit the ground like a limp, inanimate life-size doll. Life-size, but dead. The thud of smacking against the ground splashed up blood from a thousand wounds merged into one large area of torn-open skin.

"Mister, I ain't with them!" a cracked voice cried.

Edge caught a glimpse of a man standing in the firelit doorway of the assay office. He had lunged into a crouch, dropping the scattergun and scooped up the Winchester before he saw that the man had his hands clasped over his bald head.

"I live here, mister. That's all. Just live here. They come by. Asked if they could rest up for the night. That's all, mister. I ain't with them. Honest to God, I lived peaceful in Silver City all my life. I ain't—"

"Hey," Edge called easily.

"Yeah, mister?"

"I'm about convinced."

The man was in his sixties. Dressed in patched levis and a tattered shirt without a collar. He was small and

117

skinny with an emaciated face clothed in flaccid, deeply scored skin. He screwed up his eyes as if trying to prevent the tears oozing out. Some moisture dribbled from the corner of his slack mouth. As the half-breed stepped over the blasted body of Peat to advance on him, the old man seemed about to turn and run. But he held his place and, when he was close enough to look through the doorway, Edge saw why. For the same reason he had shown himself. The front entrance was the only way in and out of the assay office.

It wasn't an office anymore. Perhaps because it was the only sound building left in Silver City, the old man had turned it into a single-roomed house. There was a bed against one wall, and a table and single chair pushed against another. The fire was in a grate at the rear. There were some cooking pots, crockery and canned goods on a shelf. Nothing else.

"Name's Griffin, mister. Brad Griffin. No use me saying I'm glad to see you, on account of you'd know I was lying." He had no teeth and now his gums had started to rot. They were black and smelled bad.

Edge nodded. "Being honest pays, feller."

Griffin continued to clasp his hands over his head. "Guy took my gun. Couldn't stop him. What them young folks do to you?"

Edge spat. "Riled me."

Griffin swallowed hard. "Anything you want, you tell me, mister. I wouldn't want to get the wrong side of you."

"Stay there," the half-breed ordered, and swung around.

He ambled across the square and retrieved his own Winchester and the gunbelt. When he had buckled and tied the belt in place, he smashed Arabella's rifle against the corner of the saloon. The stock snapped away from the frame. He retraced his footsteps, and saw that the girl was still crumpled into an unconscious heap, breathing raggedly. Griffin continued to stand with his hands on his hairless head.

"They say anyone was meeting them here?"

"No, mister. Just said they was on their way to get married and asked if they could rest up here for the night. I don't own Silver City. Just live here."

"Anyone else?"

"What?"

"Live here?"

"No, mister. Just me. Been ten years since the last prospector finally gave up on digging a fortune outta the hill."

"But you're still here, uh?"

"Ain't got nowhere else to go. Lonely, but after ten years a man gets used to that. Was the blacksmith in the old days when Silver City looked like booming."

Griffin wasn't so frightened anymore. He was no longer talking to ease his nerves, rather to relieve his loneliness while he had the opportunity. The half-breed had been about to turn away; to go to hitch the team to the wagon. But suddenly he halted the movement. The abruptness of it roused Griffin's fear again.

"I say something to rile you, mister?" he stuttered.

Edge grinned. "Nothing, feller. You can take the hands down, if you want."

"Real grateful to you, mister." He lowered his hands. "Something you want?"

"To know if the forge still operates?"

Griffin expressed bewilderment. Then he shrugged. "Been better than ten years. But I could try her, I guess. You gotta horse needs shoeing?"

"Maybe that, too. I ain't checked the team."

Griffin rubbed his hands together and grinned. "Be a pleasure to do some work again." Then a crafty

119

look entered his eyes. "Talkin' of pleasure, you got anything in mind for that there girl?"

Edge looked over to where Arabella had returned to consciousness. Congealed blood was holding the two sides of the razor wound together. She was staring vacantly at the stiffening form of Walter Peat.

"Maybe."

"What?" The old man looked despondent.

"Got no money to pay you for your work."

"You mean—?" Excitement widened his eyes and erupted more moisture from the corner of his mouth.

"If you do a good job and don't care she's a little marked up, maybe you'll strike lucky in Silver City."

Griffin licked the saliva off his lips. "Ain't her face I'm interested in, mister. I ain't one to look at the mantelshelf when I'm pokin' the fire."

He gave a harsh laugh and started towards the blacksmith's forage, dragging a gimpy leg and eyeing the girl lustfully.

"No!" Arabella shrieked, the horror of the future more overwhelming than the shock of the immediate past. She struggled to rise, but was too weak from the massive loss of blood.

Edge approached her and stooped down. She cowered away from him, but he merely picked up the fallen razor. With her eyes following his every move, he crouched beside the unmoving form of Peat and cleaned the blade on the dead man's pant leg. "He only pointed a gun at me once, ma'am," the half-breed told the dumb-struck girl. "And I killed him. You did it twice, and even took a shot at me. Only right you should have a fate worse than death."

"Not with him, please!" she wailed. "Not that ugly old man!"

Edge straighened up, shrugged and showed a mirthless grin. "Way it's got to be, ma'am. I always pay my debts, but I've got no money. And Mr. Griffin is just itching to be of service."

CHAPTER EIGHT

Edge drove the wagon down from the hills in the late afternoon of the following day, while the sun was still high enough to be hot. He had slept the night in Griffin's bed at the ghost town while the old blacksmith filled his order. The trail from Silver City cut a torturous course through the high country, then ran easily through the gentler terrain lower down to connect with the main north-south route on the coast.

Since he had a rested team and a somewhat lightened wagon, the half-breed could have made better time. But he chose to match his pace with his mood. And he felt relaxed: as contented as a man like him could ever be. For he had achieved his two short-term objectives—in recovering the stolen gold and heaping brutal vengeance upon those who had taken it. The future? A man like Edge had no long-term objectives.

Yellowtown, as he approached it, did not look like the kind of place which would match his mood. The trail had taken a wide swing inland, to go around the back of a coastal hump of rock. Then it headed for the ocean again and he saw the town. Like Seascape, it was on the Oregon coast. But it was a lot closer to the Pacific breakers, which crashed angrily on one side of a strip of sand beach, as if enraged at not being able to reach the town on the other side. It had a main street which ran down to the fringe of the beach with three, narrower streets intersecting it at intervals. It was well named, for the ocean winds had lifted sand from the beach and hurled it across the town: often and forcefully enough to stain the frame buildings with its dull coloration.

There was no wind today, as the team and the wagon wheels left their prints in the mantel of sand layered on the street. The impressions were super-imposed on many others, for Yellowtown had had some heavy traffic. And all of it had been one way. Down at the intersection closest to the beach, the main street was blocked with double-parked wagons; covered rigs, flatbeds, buckboards and buggies. Saddle horses were hitched to every available rail and post. People—men, women and children, thronged the sidewalks and streets.

Beyond the intersection, Edge could see on to the beach, where the carny tents had been set up. But there was not a customer nor a spieler to be seen among the tents with their garishly painted signs. And the half-breed could recognize no familiar figure in the crowd at the intersection, whose interest was centered upon one of the buildings on the south side of the street. It seemed like an angry interest.

But not every citizen of Yellowtown was down at the ocean end of the street. The lone figure of a middle-aged woman stood, arms akimbo, in the doorway of The Ocean Spray Restaurant in the middle of the block between the first and center intersection.

She had a thin body and a haggard face. Her soured expression seemed like a permanent fixture. It became even more deeply inscribed into her sallow complexion when Edge angled the wagon to the side of the street and reined the team to a halt immediately outside the restaurant. Her bleak eyes raked from the driver, to the tiger show sign on the ripped canvas, then back to the driver.

"I don't want no trouble in my place," she announced, and her voice matched her looks.

"What about custom?" Edge asked, picking up the Winchester and climbing down to the sidewalk.

"From you people, that means trouble," she answered, and unfolded her arms to jerk a thumb down the street. "Look what's happening at the Pacific Winds Hotel."

He could look west without screwing up his eyes now, for the sun had changed color from blazing yellow to dull red as its leading arc reached for the top of the ocean's curve. He spat under the belly of one of the horses in the wagon traces.

You can tell me all about it while I'm eating, ma'am," he said, and brushed past the woman to enter the restaurant.

The room was neat and clean, with a dozen tables set in four place settings on red and white gingham cloths. Automatically, Edge selected a table where he could sit with his back to a wall and have a clear view of doors and windows. He leaned the rifle against the chair and hooked his hat over the muzzle.

"Steak and the trimmings," he said. "No soup to start. And no dessert if the steak's as big as I hope it's going to be."

The sour-faced woman had watched him irately. She seemed about to yell at him, but then she came inside and shrugged her shoulders. "Since you're the only customer I reckon I'll get today, I might as well make the most of you."

She slouched between the tables and went out through a door at the rear. Edge rolled a cigarette and smoked it. The appetizing smell of cooking meat wafted into the restaurant through the doorway into which the woman had gone. Vishwabandhu Nageshwar Singh came in through the door from the street. He was dressed to do his show, in a sweatstained loincloth and with a tiger skin draped over his shoulders. His ribs ridged the dark skin of his naked chest and his legs looked like thin lengths of brown timber. His eyes and teeth glinted with excitement.

"Did I not tell them, sahib!" he exclaimed. "I told them you would most certainly recover the big gold."

The half-breed grinned at the little Nepalese as he weaved between the tables. "Where's the cats, feller?"

Singh halted before the table and his expression became crestfallen. "Oh dear, dear me! The sheriff of this town. A most severe man named de Cruz. He make me lock my beautiful beasts in livery stable. Not allow me to show them until they in cage. Not believe they most amenable tigers, sahib." He brightened. "But now is okay, goodness gracious. You bring back my cage. Just like I tell Mr. Case you would, sahib. I watch for you all day. That how I see you come to Yellowtown. While all the others cower in hotel, fearful of people's anger."

The woman emerged from the kitchen, carrying a plate of food. She saw Singh and pulled up sharply. "Oh, Christ, another one of 'em," she wailed.

Edge nodded. "Like I told him before, ma'am, his crowd's getting everywhere these days."

"How'd you get out of the hotel?" she asked Singh as she started forward to deliver the plate to the table.

125

"I am most clever Nepalese, lady," Singh answered. "Small, too. I climb out of window everyone think too little to guard."

"You want grub?"

"Thank you, no. I am too excited to eat now that everything going to be all right. The sahib has brought back big gold."

The woman had been about to return to her vantage point at the doorway. But she pulled up short, and stared hard at Edge as he began to eat the meal.

"Good," he told her.

"But can't it wait until after you've delivered what you brought?" she demanded. "I didn't know you were the guy they've been waiting for. Christ, there could be a lynching while you're sitting here filling your belly!"

Edge continued to chew on the succulent beef.

"Lady right, sahib!" Singh urged. "Lots of bills put up all over countryside. Promising big gold worth one million dollars to be seen in Yellowtown. People come many miles to see it. When get here and no gold to see, they very very angry. Goodness gracious, how angry they are. Blame Mr. Case most, but not like any show people. Not want to see my beautiful beasts or anything. Want only to tear down our tents and maybe beat us. But most severe sheriff de Cruz, he order us into hotel. For protection, you understand."

"But he's only one man," the woman pointed out. "And there's some real tough guys live in Yellowtown and out on the farms. Hard drinkers, and they been drinking, mister. Getting meaner with every drink they took."

"And I've been getting hungrier every mile I've covered," the half-breed responded.

There was a shout out on the street, strident above the distant buzz of angry conversation. The woman groaned and hurried to the doorway. Her body became rigid as she looked out. All the sourness in every fiber of her emaciated body showed in her face as she glowered back over her shoulder. "Didn't I tell you," she accused. "Didn't I say you'd bring trouble to my place?" She sighed. "They've seen your wagon."

Edge hooked the hat from over the Winchester muzzle and set it on his head. Then he sighed, stood up and sloped the Winchester across his shoulder.

"Oh dear, dear me," Singh muttered.

"I don't want no shooting in my place, mister!" the woman warned.

Edge looked down reflectively at his half eaten meal, then started towards the door. "I'll go along with you there, ma'am," he said. "There's more than enough noise for a man to eat by with your voice."

"You can always eat someplace else," she flung at him as he pushed past her.

He grinned. "Doubt if there's a better steak to be had in town."

The spontaneous flattery held the sour-faced woman in a surprised silence. Then the frontrunners of the angry crowd reached the restaurant, spreading in a tight-packed half circle around the parked wagon. They were noisy, until they became aware of the menacing nonchalance of the tall half-breed standing in the doorway, Winchester canted easily across his shoulder.

"Oh dear, dear me!" Singh muttered, ducking behind Edge as he saw so many pairs of eyes watching him, their massed threat seeming to become more powerful as the noise faded.

"It's the wagon!" a woman yelled. "Look, you can see the bars where the canvas's torn."

127

"Let's see if it's inside!' a man responded, and started to climb up on to the seat.

"Make way there! Make way!"

Edge saw the barrel-chested man with a shot of red hair atop a red face elbowing his way through from the rear of the crowd. He saw the silver badge on his check shirt.

"Sheriff de Cruz," Singh said fearfully.

Edge flicked his wrist and extended his free hand. The Winchester fell forward and the action slapped against his cupped palm. He pumped a shell into the breech and squeezed the trigger. The bullet bit into the wagon seat, spitting splinters. The man climbing aboard vented a cry of alarm and fell back. Blood beaded from the center of his cheek where a fragment of wood had punctured the skin.

"Hold it right there!" de Cruz roared, bursting clear of the press and climbing up on to the sidewalk. He toted an old Henry repeater rifle. Its muzzle pointing skywards and he squeezed the trigger. The second shot silenced the buzz of talk started by the first. "What the hell's happening?"

"Guy blasted me, sheriff!" the superficially injured man accused, rubbing at his cheek with a dirty handkerchief.

"I saw!" de Cruz growled, and swung towards Edge. The half-breed had adopted a relaxed pose again after pumping the action a second time. "What's the idea?"

"Wagon don't belong to me, feller," he answered. "But I'm taking care of it. Object to rubbernecks climbing all over it."

The lawman glanced at the wagon, and did a double-take at the lettering and pictures on the side. "Hey, that's the black's wagon!" Then he took an-

128

other, longer look at Edge. "The one the carny people reckon was loaded with gold."

"And some of them said the sahib stole!" Singh said emphatically, stepping out from behind the half-breed. "Didn't I say he bring it back?"

"Take a look inside, sheriff!" the injured man demanded. "He won't stop you."

Edge's Winchester was across his shoulder again, but de Cruz held back from moving.

"I aim to, mister," the lawman growled, addressing the half-breed. "Some of these here folks have come a long way, and lost a day's work to see this crazy big gold show. I gotta be sure they're gonna get what they came for. And if they ain't, I'm not gonna be held responsible for the consequences."

"Singh?" Edge said softly into the tense silence which trailed the sheriff's ultimatum.

"Yes, sahib?"

"Can the sheriff take a look inside your wagon?"

"Oh, goodness gracious, most certainly he can, sahib," the little Nepalese replied quickly. "I wish for no trouble with lawman or anybody else. Oh dear, dear me, no."

"Go ahead," Edge invited.

"Was going to anyway," de Cruz growled, and hauled himself up on to the seat.

There was more shouting from down at the main intersection and Edge looked in that direction, across the heads of the expectant crowd. A group of the carny people had emerged from the no-longer beseiged Pacific Winds Hotel and were running towards the large gathering in front of the restaurant. They were led by Roger Case and Jo Jo Lamont.

The sheriff withdrew his head from peering into the wagon and emitted a disconcerted grunt. "I don't see no gold, mister!" he said with menace.

129

The murmuring of massed anger rose from the press of people again. The majority of the group which had come from the hotel halted and did a fast about-face to retrace their footsteps. After the others had returned to their sanctuary, only Case and Jo Jo remained in the open.

"Ain't no free show, feller," Edge told the glowering lawman. "You pay your fifty cents at the proper time and place, and you'll see the big gold."

"You got it, Edge?" Case yelled.

Edge spat under the belly of the horse. "You hired me to do a job," he replied. "Wouldn't have taken it if I didn't intend to do it."

"I don't see it aboard the wagon!" de Cruz growled, addressing Case.

The dudishly dressed man took a backward step as all eyes swung towards him. Jo Jo looked confused.

"But you've got it someplace, Edge?"

The half-breed nodded. The sun touched the horizon and was suddenly a deeper shade of red. The color suffused the whole town.

"Near by?"

"Close enough."

"When can it go on show?"

"Soon as you like."

"Say an hour to set it up down on the site?"

"Why not." The half-breed shrugged and turned to reenter the restaurant.

"That all right with you, sheriff?" he heard Case ask as he returned to his table at the rear of the room and sat down.

"The folks have waited this long," de Cruz muttered with ill-humor. "Guess another hour won't make much difference. You just be sure to deliver, mister."

There was a ripple of angry agreement, and then a

shuffling of feet as the crowd dispersed. Edge continued with his meal, watched by the happy Singh and the bewildered woman. Then footfalls sounded on the sidewalk and Case led Jo Jo into the restaurant.

"Hell, Edge, I thought you was gone for sure," the dude rasped, jerking a chair away from a table and flopping down into it.

"Try to find me in the bottom of a bottle?" the half-breed asked, looking at the bloodshot eyes in the pale face and noticing the way Case's hands trembled.

"I was damn worried!" the owner of the gold snapped waspishly. "What was I to think damn it? You take off hell-for-leather with the big gold. Then Peat and his girl go chasing off. Said they were going after you to help you, but they wouldn't take me or Jo Jo along. Then, when the Nep—"

"His name is Singh!" Edge cut in.

"All right. All right. When he came back with just his tigers, I had some more crazy thoughts. Then we got here and the crowd turned ugly. I needed to get some comfort somehow."

Edge finished his steak and pushed his plate away. "Fine cooking, ma'am," he complimented the sour-faced woman, who looked almost coy in response. Then he began to pick at his teeth with a match as he eyed Jo Jo. "Seems to me you were ready to help him in that department?"

The girl flushed. "Mr. Case thinks he can use me to take the cash, that's all. No strings attached."

"Maybe as a guard, too. The way you handle a rifle."

"I was brought up in Arizona Territory, Mr. Edge. Apache country. Everyone learns to shoot good down there, I can tell you."

131

"What the hell does it matter?" Case snarled, shooting to his feet from the chair. "Where's the gold so we can put on the show before all hell breaks loose?"

"How much for the food, ma'am?" the half-breed asked as he rose, putting on his hat and lifting the rifle.

"Dollar even."

Edge dropped a bill on the table beside the plate and stood up. She took the money and the plate and went into the kitchen.

"Do we have to haul it far?" Case asked anxiously, snatching a look at a pocket watch.

Edge took a napkin from the table nearest the door as he went out, followed by the dude, the Nepalese and the girl. "End of the street, is all."

Bewilderment showed on the trio of faces as Edge climbed up on to the wagon seat and pulled aside the front flap of the canvas covering. The entire crowd had moved away and were divided between the down-town saloons and the carny site, where some of the spielers were attracting an audience for their shows. Thus, only the four outside the restaurant saw the row of black bars exposed by the open flap.

"The sheriff said you didn't have it aboard!" Case snapped.

"Only natural a sheriff wouldn't take much notice of bars," the half-breed answered. He spat again, this time on the napkin. Then he used the damp square of linen to rub at one of the bars. The thin coating of soot from the Silver City forge came off easily, to reveal the rich luster of gold beneath.

"Goodness gracious me," Singh gasped.

"Wow!" Jo Jo exclaimed.

"Why?" Case wanted to know.

"Hoped to talk you out of doing any more shows,"

132

Edge answered, allowing the flap to drop back into place and conceal the camouflaged golden cage. "Been easier to get the gold to someplace safe like this. But your audience has got a more powerful argument than I have."

Case licked his pale lips. "It'll be the last show, Edge," he said emphatically. "Even if I lose, I can't stand the strain anymore."

"Lose what?" Jo Jo asked, intrigued.

Case shook his head. "That's my business!"

Singh eyed the wagon despondently. "Gold cage no use to put my beautiful tigers in. Will not hold them if they become no longer amenable. Gold bars bend, I am thinking."

"You're still on eight dollars a day," the half-breed reminded him as he climbed down to the sidewalk.

"Goodness gracious, yes," the Nepalese exclaimed, grinning happily again.

Jo Jo was blushing under the scrutiny of Roger Case, who raked her from head to toe and back again with anxious eyes as he chewed on his nails. Then he grunted and grinned.

"I've got an idea!" he rasped.

"From you, that's got to be bad," Edge said wryly.

"What is as good to look at as gold?" the dude demanded, ignoring the sarcasm.

"Tigers, I think," Singh replied.

"No!" Case snapped. "Women. Combine the two and it's perfect. You won't be taking money at the front of the tent, Miss Lamont."

"I won't?"

"No you'll be inside, as part of the show. In the costume you wore when you worked with Turk. Scanty. You displaying your charms in the cage. A pairing of the two things men want most out of life." He snapped his fingers. "Wait." He pointed one finger

133

at Singh. "And you. You will play music."

"For extra to my eight dollars, sahib?"

Case ignored the request for a raise. "Miss Lamont will dance."

The girl swallowed hard. "I don't know," she said hesitantly.

Case was already climbing aboard the wagon. Singh went up on to the seat beside him. The girl stood on the sidewalk, looking nervously around her. She gulped again.

"What do you think, Mr. Edge?" she asked.

"Come on, Miss Lamont," Case urged, ignoring everything else as he became increasingly excited about his idea. "Time is running out."

"He's right," the half-breed agreed.

"Then you think I ought to—"

Edge nodded. "Go go, Jo Jo."

CHAPTER NINE

Edge watched Case's new show and reflected that Mrs. Blackhouse would not have approved. Not many of the women who lived in Yellowtown and out in the surrounding countryside approved either. They showed their disdain by boycotting the big wedge tent with the new sign outside the entrance: SEE JO JO LAMONT DANCE IN THE GOLDEN CAGE WORTH $1,000,000. ADMISSION $1.

Case did not lose by the boycott, and not simply because he had doubled his charge. For he did a great deal of repeat business, as men emerged at the conclusion of one performance and then joined the back of the line to see another. Also, Case was in favor with his fellow showmen for the first time since joining the carny. For the women and children, denied the opportunity of seeing the big gold, went instead to the other tents flanking the midway on the beach. As the sun plunged to a crimson death in the ocean and a star-sprinkled, brightly moonlit night descended on the Oregon coast, the whole carny bustled. The rubber man, the bearded lady, the red-nosed clown, the fortune teller and every other side-show did boom business.

But no audience was more appreciative than that which cheered, whistled and applauded throughout and at the conclusion of each show by Jo Jo Lamont. Edge watched two of the ten minute shows, standing at the rear of the crowd, just inside the tent entrance. The little Nepalese, still clothed in a loincloth and tiger skin, squatted on the roof of the cage, which still rested on the wagon with its cover removed and tail-gate and sides dropped. The kerosene lamps had been carefully placed, one at each corner of the cage, which had been wiped clean of the soot. Placed so that they caused the golden bars to glow with a rich sheen and, equally important, shone to good effect on Jo Jo Lamont's writhing flesh.

And there was a lot of her flesh for the light to shine on. Of her own accord, or perhaps upon the insistence of Roger Case, the girl was even more scantily clad than when she had been the human target for Turk's knives. She wore no hose in the cage, and had undertaken some rapid alterations to the red and blue tunic: cutting away the midsection and turning over hems so that she was clothed only in a strip of blue encircling her hips and an equally spartan strip of red cradling her full breasts. Thus, as she flung her body about in frenetic movement to match the pace of Singh's uptempo harmonica music, there was little of her body not on view to the delighted eyes of the all-male audience.

Jo Jo was not so elegant as Arabella had been, but elegance had no place in this show. She was a near-naked woman moving through a hundred variations of erotic actions designed to excite the men watching

136

l er. The frantic music and the glistening bars were additional stimulants. And, most sexually intoxicating of all, it was blatantly obvious that Jo Jo was enjoying the show as much as any man watching her.

"Going well, uh Edge?" the beaming Case said as the half-breed stepped out of the tent ahead of the delighted audience at the conclusion of the second performance. "Not such a bad idea after all?"

Edge nodded. "Years ahead of its time, I reckon."

He waited until the last man had emerged from the tent and Case began to collect the admission money from the new audience. Coins and bills were eagerly handed over and dropped by the dude into the tin box on the table at which he sat.

"Mind telling me what it's all about now, feller?"

Case continued to nod his thanks to each man who gave him a dollar. "Investment. Return on capital. High finance. I'm just a simple businessman."

Edge leaned forward to peer into the cash box, stuffed almost full with money. "Not so simple, I guess."

"That's all for now, folks," Case called, and released a rope which dropped the flap over the tent entrance. The line halted reluctantly and Singh started to play his mouth organ, beginning in a low key and then building up to the climax. The audience roared its approval. "You've altered your opinion of me, Edge?" He turned to look at the half-breed now, and broadened his smile to a beaming grin.

Edge responded with a quiet smile that curled back his lips but did not reach his hooded eyes. "Guess a smart feller can do crazy things sometimes," he allowed. "Especially where money's concerned. I could have been doing something easy like felling redwoods. But the finance wouldn't have been so high."

He hefted the Winchester and started along the side

137

of the tent. As he turned the rear corner, a trio of young boys—no more than twelve—sprang away from a split in the canvas. The towering figure of the lean half-breed held them rooted to the spot by fear.

"Gee, mister!" one of them blurted out.

"Beat it," Edge told them softly.

They whirled, and were halted again, by the sight of a broad, stumpy woman.

"Mom!"

"Home!" she yelled at them. "This minute." Then she looked at Edge and sniffed. "At least one of you people cares about the corrupting of young minds," she said stiffly.

"Ain't that, ma'am," he told her. "But they want to see the show, they got to pay the same as everyone else."

"Well, I never!" she snorted, swinging around to shepherd her sons away.

"Wouldn't appeal to you," Edge said to her retreating figure.

The crack of gunfire was like an unexpected thunderclap from a brilliantly blue sky. At least a dozen guns, Edge guessed, as he whirled towards the corner of the tent. Rifles. Fired on the street. Close by. At the beach end, where the carny midway was set up. The sounds of people enjoying themselves faltered. A second fusillade exploded and almost every sound was silenced. Except for the harmonica music from within the tent.

"Stop the friggin' music!" a man bellowed.

"Quit it, nigger!" a man inside the tent demanded.

The music stopped. "Oh dear, dear me," Singh muttered.

"This is a friggin' stick up!"

Edge halted at the corner and peered along the side

138

of the tent. Once more, not that it mattered tonight, Case had claimed the prime position for his show. The tent was pitched at the very end of the street, just where the hard-packed dirt with its covering of loose sand gave way to the beach. Thus, the half-breed had a clear view of the brightly-lit downtown section, as far as the nearest intersection. Beyond this, Yellowtown had closed up for the night and the empty street was lit only by silvered moonlight. But the moon was sufficiently bright for the narrowed eyes of Edge to see a familiar shape. A buggy drawn by a white horse was moving slowly along the street towards the lighted strip. The driver was not yet discernible against the dark interior of the buggy. But he knew it was the fat Clarence French who held the reins.

"We blast anybody and everybody who don't friggin' well do what we friggin' well tell you!"

The fat man was not shouting the orders. This voice came from the wrong direction, and did not have French's cultured tones. The man was shouting from a rooftop on the south side of the street. Edge looked up at him and, like everybody else among the tents, saw the man was not alone. He was standing, silhouetted against the night sky, aiming a rifle from the shoulder. Eight other men were up there in identical stances. Edge swung his gaze to the opposite side of the street and counted six other figures skylined on a roof top.

"Do like they say," Sheriff de Cruz yelled from the far side of the carny.

The white gelding drew the buggy across the intersection and lamplight shafted into its interior to reveal the obese form of Clarence French.

"You sure don't give up easy," the half-breed rasped softly as he backed away from the corner of the tent. He turned and moved forward in a crouching run, then changed course and ducked into the shadows of a building. He slowed his pace now that there was hard-packed dirt beneath his feet instead of the muffling sand of the beach.

"Gent's comin' down the friggin' street," the man yelled from the roof top. "Gonna park his friggin' buggy and wait awhile. He don't like waitin'." He spat. "So you, sheriff, and a couple of other guys better be friggin' quick in hitchin' up a team to that big gold wagon. Get me?"

"You can't let them do it!" Case bellowed.

"Shuddup!" de Cruz snarled. "Harley, Church! Get a team for the wagon!"

Case, the crimson of anger spreading to swamp his pale complexion, reached into his coat for the pepperbox. As the two designated men moved to the remuda for the horses, another man emerged from the tent and slammed a vicious chop across the dude's wrist. The multi-barrelled handgun thudded to the ground.

"I got a wife and four kids out there in front of the guns," the attacker snarled.

Edge looked down a narrow alley between a bank and a hardware store. He had a clear shot of the fat man as French reined the gelding to a halt on the opposite side of the street.

"We ain't friggin' kiddin', de Cruz!" the man on the roof warned.

"Know you ain't!" the sheriff answered. "I'll hang any man starts trouble."

French was smiling as he put down the reins and caressed the ivory butts of his matched revolvers. "The young lady," he called up to the roof of the office building outside which he was parked.

"Oh, yeah," the man transmitting his orders muttered, then raised his voice. "Somethin' else, de Cruz. Like the dame to stay inside the cage."

Edge moved on, parallel with the street, across the rear of the buildings on the north side. Once across the side street forming the downtown intersection, he went faster. He halted just once, at the rear of the livery. From inside came the soft purring of Singh's tigers. Then they caught his scent and gave low growls. Edge scooped up a coil of rope and continued towards the midtown intersection.

The man who had knocked the pepperbox from Case's hand now held a revolver against the dude's back. Seething with impotent anger, Case watched while de Cruz, Harley and Church tore down the tent from over the wagon.

"Goodness gracious me, this is most unfortunate," Singh muttered as the gold case aboard the wagon was exposed to the frightened eyes of the non-paying audience.

"Get off the top of the wagon, nigger," de Cruz ordered.

"I am not nigger, sahib!" the Nepalese protested. "Colored."

"You'll be red-spotted, you don't do like I say," the lawman snarled.

Singh leapt down to the sand.

"Please?" was all Jo Jo was able to force out through her terror-dried mouth as a four horse team was backed up to the wagon.

"You're a stranger in town, lady," de Cruz growled. "My first duty is to protect the local folk."

The girl turned her fear-filled eyes away from the shocked watchers. She saw the massive Clarence French step out of his buggy and start to waddle across the beach. She recalled what had been in her mind two nights ago and she shuddered. For the fat

141

man's good humor took the form of a leer now: an evil expression coveting the gold and the woman. Jo Jo sank to the floor of the cage and tried to cover herself.

Oozing confidence, French waddled through the space left by the crowd and hauled his bulk up on the wagon. "I thank you, sheriff," he said. "Apologies to you, Case. Very pleased you expressed a wish to accompany me, Miss Lamont. Craig, are you coming?"

The clown, with a red nose and a whitened face and dressed in a baggy, multi-colored costume, emerged from the press of people. His mouth, enlarged out of proportion by carefully applied greasepaint, showed a broad grin as he hefted himself into a sitting posture on the rear of the wagon. "You!" Case accused.

"Funny, ain't it?" the clown said, and giggled.

"My men will retire as soon as I am clear," French promised, his bulbous features continuing to express good humor. "I should be most happy if there was no further bloodshed on account of the gold."

"There won't be!" de Cruz said emphatically, glaring at Case.

Jo Jo began to sob. French flicked the reins across the backs of the team and the wagon rolled forward. Slow on the beach, but picking up speed as the hooves and wheels found the firmer ground of the street surface. The large crowd on the sand watched its departure. The men on the roof tops watched the crowd on the sand. The wagon gathered more speed, hurtling across the lighted intersection.

"Where the hell is Edge?" Case snarled, raking his eyes across the faces of the crowd as French galloped the team along the darkened stretch of street.

"They're leavin'!" a woman shouted.

Staring eyes switched direction from the street to

142

he rooftops. The woman was half right. The men on the top of the hardware store were climbing down— on to the stoop roof and then leaping to the street. They ran across to disappear along the side of office building. The nine other men remained on the roof covering the retreat of those below. Then they whirled, raced to the rear of the building and thudded down the outside stairway to where their horses were waiting.

"Get after them!" Case shrieked.

The gun dug harder into his back.

"Shuddup!" the sheriff snarled, anxious eyes searching for a sight of the men while his ears strained to catch the hoofbeats of their flight. But, the moment the men yelled at their mounts to urge them into speed, another explosion of noise erupted.

Edge was crouched on the stoop roof of a house beyond the uptown intersection, directly opposite The Ocean Spray Restaurant. The house and the restaurant were both darkened and empty. Just below him, one end of the rope was lashed to a pole supporting the stoop roof. The rope stretched tautly away from him, the other end secured to a post supporting the sidewalk awning outside the restaurant. The distance between the rope and street surface was about eight feet: chest high to the fat man on the seat of the wagon.

The half-breed was unaware of events at the beach end of the street. After setting up the rope barrier, he had concentrated his entire attention upon the wagon. Now, as French continued to lash and yell at the team, racing across the last intersection, Edge levelled the Winchester, swinging it to keep aim on the fat man.

He saw the evil joy change abruptly to fear on the bulbous, sheened features. And he knew French had

143

seen the black line of the rope. Only forty feet separated the wagon from the rope. The fat man hauled on the reins and reached for the brake lever, a scream of terror venting from his gaping mouth. Then he saw there was not a chance. He hefted his bulky body, swinging to the side to leap from the hurtling wagon. Edge squeezed the trigger. Then he powered into a leap of his own.

It was over in a matter of stretched seconds. The bullet drove into French's massive body, tunneling through layers of fat to tear into his heart. The man sat down hard on the seat, his back crashing into the golden bars. Jo Jo Lamont screamed. The clown only had time to turn his head at the shot. Then the team galloped under the rope, which hooked beneath French's neck as the fat man slumped into death. The horses were still racing at full speed. Posts, rope and human flesh and bone—something had to give. The posts creaked and the rope stretched. The fat man's head and shoulders were forced against the golden bars.

The cage slid backwards. The clown and Jo Jo screamed. The cage gathered speed. The clown was swept off the rear of the wagon and his scream ended. He hit the street hard with his skull and a sharp crack as his neck broke. The floor of the golden cage fouled the hinges of the tailgate. Then tore through them. Both the posts snapped and the rope parted at the same time. The cage shot off the rear of the wagon, the soft metal crumpling as it crashed to the street. The wagon hurtled onwards. The fat man toppled off the seat and bounced to the ground, his head half-severed by the no-longer taut rope. Something red, blue and flesh-colored was tossed through the crumpled bars of the gold cage. It sailed through the ir and thudded to a soft landing on the inert form of the clown.

Then there was just the sound of racing wheels and thudding hoofbeats. After the cacophany of creaking, tearing, screaming, crashing, wrenching and cracking sounds, the diminishing noise of the racing wagon was almost restful. But more than four horses were pumping their hooves into the Oregon ground.

Edge, still in a crouch from the jump just before the stoop roof collapsed with the snapping of the support, powered forward. He hitched out full-length behind the large heap of French's dead body. He rested the Winchester on the bulging belly, aiming towards the inland end of the street.

French's men had galloped their mounts in a half circle around the southern side of Yellowtown. They reined the snorting animals to a halt as the bolting, driverless team hauled the empty wagon clear of the street and on to the trail.

The Winchester exploded and a man left his saddle, pouring blood from a wound in the side of his head. The rifle cracked again as the horsemen snapped their attention from the wagon to stare down the street. A second man hit the ground, screaming and clutching at his stomach. The men saw the crumpled golden cage and the three slumped, unmoving forms. Then they saw the muzzle flash of the Winchester as it fired a third shot from the cover of the fat man. Death struck a third time, the victim taking the bullet in the heart. He slumped forward, staying in the saddle.

"We're bein' slaughtered!" somebody yelled, and swung his rifle.

His shot was the first of a barrage. Edge pressed his face into the sandy ground. Bullets thudded into the

145

unfeeling flesh of the fat man and buried into the gold.

"Let's rope her and drag her!"

"It's an idea, I reckon we . . ."

The voice faded as an explosion of noise sounded at the far end of the street. Shouting and then a barrage of gunfire. Bullets whined over Edge's head.

"No friggin' chance!"

"Let's get!"

The half-breed raised his head and sighted the rifle as the men wheeled their horses. He got off two more shots and saw crimson blossom on toppling forms. Then the men were out of sight, hidden by the row of buildings on the south side of the street. The sound of their retreat faded, then was swamped by the thudding of massed footfalls. Edge picked himself up. He dusted the sand off his shirt and pants as he looked coldly at the dead men sprawled where the street met the open trail. Then he turned to give the same impassive examination to French, the clown and Jo Jo Lamont, sprawled at either side of the crumpled cage, the twisted gold bars glinting in the moonlight. Finally, he surveyed the crowd, which had halted and become silent on the fringe of the scene of carnage.

"Oh dear, dear me!" Singh muttered, shaking his head, his brown face wreathed by sadness. "The desire for riches can indeed have most unfortunate consequences."

Sheriff de Cruz was standing beside the little Nepalese, dwarfing him. He glowered meanly at Edge. "If just one local citizen had been killed, you'd have hung, mister!" he rasped.

The half-breed was reloading the Winchester. He didn't have enough shells to completely fill the magazine. "You had your job to do, feller," he said softly. "Mine was to keep the gold from being stole."

146

The dudishly attired Case stood on the other side of the lawman, his smallness of stature also made blatant by de Cruz's bulk. He seemed to shrink even more as he moved away from the forefront of silent, shocked crowd. He went to where the near-naked girl was draped over the broken body of the painted clown. Edge moved around the golden cage to stand on the other side of the slumped forms.

"She's still breathing!" Case gasped.

The hooded eyes of the half-breed showed no emotion as they watched the almost imperceptible rise and fall of Jo Jo's half-exposed breasts.

"Nothing's ever all bad," he said.

"Except my ideas," Case groaned.

"Next time, see an investment broker," the half-breed suggested wryly.

"Like my brother did," Case murmured. "My father gave us a quarter of a million dollars each. Whichever of us gets the highest return on capital over six months will get the balance of his estate. Ten million dollars. I was doing fine."

"From now on, you do it without me, feller," Edge told him. "Job's ended as far as I'm concerned. The whole thing was crazy from the start. The fat man getting killed won't stop them. They're gonna try for the gold every inch of the way. I ain't pushing my luck no further."

Case straightened up, pulling some bills from inside his expensive jacket. Tears gleamed in the corners of his eyes and he kept the lids far apart, as if afraid to squeeze the wetness out. He thrust the money at Edge.

"You're right. Take the full hundred. You earned it. I never thought all this would happen."

The half-breed accepted the sheaf of money, counted off fifty dollars and handed the remainder back to Case. "Two nights and a day," he said. "Whatever that adds up to plus my expenses. I've used a lot of shells."

Case took the bills automatically and looked at them for a long time, as if trying to decide what they were. Then his tear-filled eyes met the cool stare of the half-breed. "I was right about you. You are an honest man. And you aren't greedy either."

Edge showed a cold grin. "If I ever need a reference, I'll know who to come to." He glanced down at the bodies of Jo Jo and the clown. The girl had stopped breathing now and her face showed a serene innocence in death.

Case looked at the girl and recognized the meaning of her utter stillness. "All for this," he said, clenching his fist around the bills. A single tear squeezed from each eye and coursed down his wan cheeks. "So many people have died just because I wanted a lot of this," More tears now, of mixed anger and sorrow as he released the money and bills fluttered to the street. "It's mad!"

"Lots of people die," Edge said. "All the time. A lot of them for this." He held up his own money, then pushed it into a shirt pocket.

"Mad!" the dude croaked. "It was a crazy thing to do."

"Yeah," the half-breed agreed, glancing down a final time at the innocent girl sprawled across the grotesquely dressed and painted clown. "Virgin on the ridiculous."

148

THE EXECUTIONER
by Don Pendleton

WARBOTS by G. Harry Stine

#5 OPERATION HIGH DRAGON   (17-159, $3.95)

Civilization is under attack! A "virus program" has been injected into America's polar-orbit military satellites by an unknown enemy. The only motive can be the preparation for attack against the free world. The source of "infection" is traced to a barren, storm-swept rock-pile in the southern Indian Ocean. Now, it is up to the forces of freedom to search out and destroy the enemy. With the aid of their robot infantry—the Warbots—the Washington Greys mount Operation High Dragon in a climactic battle for the future of the free world.

#6 THE LOST BATTALION   (17-205, $3.95)

Major Curt Carson has his orders to lead his Warbot-equipped Washington Greys in a search-and-destroy mission in the mountain jungles of Borneo. The enemy: a strongly entrenched army of Shiite Muslim guerrillas who have captured the Second Tactical Battalion, threatening them with slaughter. As allies, the Washington Greys have enlisted the Grey Lotus Battalion, a mixed-breed horde of Japanese jungle fighters. Together with their newfound allies, the small band must face swarming hordes of fanatical Shiite guerrillas in a battle that will decide the fate of Southeast Asia and the security of the free world.

#7 OPERATION IRON FIST   (17-253, $3.95)

Russia's centuries-old ambition to conquer lands along its southern border erupts in a savage show of force that pits a horde of Soviet-backed Turkish guerrillas against the freedom-loving Kurds in their homeland high in the Caucasus Mountains. At stake: the rich oil fields of the Middle East. Facing certain annihilation, the valiant Kurds turn to the robot infantry of Major Curt Carson's "Ghost Forces" for help. But the brutal Turks far outnumber Carson's desperately embattled Washington Greys, and on the blood-stained slopes of historic Mount Ararat, the high-tech warriors of tomorrow must face their most awesome challenge yet!

MYSTIC REBEL by Ryder Syvertsen

MYSTIC REBEL (17-104, $3.95)

It was duty that first brought CIA operative Bart Lasker to the mysterious frozen mountains of Tibet. But a deeper obligation made him remain behind, disobeying orders to wage a personal war against the brutal Red Chinese oppressors.

MYSTIC REBEL II (17-079, $3.95)

Conscience first committed CIA agent Bart Lasker to Tibet's fight for deliverance from the brutal yoke of Red Chinese oppression. But a strange and terrible power bound the unsuspecting American to the mysterious kingdom—freeing the Western avenger from the chains of mortality, transforming him from mere human to the MYSTIC REBEL!

MYSTIC REBEL III (17-141, $3.95)

At the bidding of the Dalai Lama, the Mystic Rebel must return to his abandoned homeland to defend a newborn child. The infant's life-spark is crucial to the survival of the ancient mountain people—but forces of evil have vowed that the child shall die at birth.

MYSTIC REBEL IV (17-232, $3.95)

Nothing short of death at the hands of his most dreaded enemies—the Bonpo magicians, worshippers of the Dark One—will keep the legendary warrior from his chosen destiny—a life or death struggle in the labyrinthine depths of the Temple of the Monkey God, where the ultimate fate of a doomed world hangs in the balance!

ESPIONAGE FICTION BY WARREN MURPHY AND MOLLY COCHRAN

GRANDMASTER (17-101, $4.50)
There are only two true powers in the world. One is goodness. One is evil. And one man knows them both. He knows the uses of pleasure, the secrets of pain. He understands the deadly forces that grip the world in treachery. He moves like a shadow, a promise of danger, from Moscow to Washington—from Havana to Tibet. In a game that may never be over, he is the grandmaster.

THE HAND OF LAZARUS (17-100, $4.50)
A grim spectre of death looms over the tiny County Kerry village of Ardath. The savage plague of urban violence has begun to weave its insidious way into the peaceful fabric of Irish country life. The IRA's most mysterious, elusive, and bloodthirsty murderer has chosen Ardath as his hunting ground, the site that will rock the world and plunge the beleaguered island nation into irreversible chaos: the brutal assassination of the Pope.

Available wherever paperbacks are sold, or order direct from the Publisher. Send cover price plus 50¢ per copy for mailing and handling to Pinnacle Books, Dept. 17-331, 475 Park Avenue South, New York, N.Y. 10016. Residents of New York, New Jersey and Pennsylvania must include sales tax. DO NOT SEND CASH.

ED MCBAIN'S MYSTERIES

JACK AND THE BEANSTALK   (17-083, $3.95)
Jack's dead, stabbed fourteen times. And thirty-six thousand's missing in cash. Matthew's questions are turning up some long-buried pasts, a second dead body, and some beautiful suspects. Like Sunny, Jack's sister, a surfer boy's fantasy, a delicious girl with some unsavory secrets.

BEAUTY AND THE BEAST   (17-134, $3.95)
She was spectacular—an unforgettable beauty with exquisite features. On Monday, the same woman appeared in Hope's law office to file a complaint. She had been badly beaten—a mass of purple bruises with one eye swollen completely shut. And she wanted her husband put away before something worse happened. Her body was discovered on Tuesday, bound with wire coat hangers and burned to a crisp. But her husband—big, and monstrously ugly—denies the charge.

Available wherever paperbacks are sold, or order direct from the Publisher. Send cover price plus 50¢ per copy for mailing and handling to Pinnacle Books, Dept. 17-331, 475 Park Avenue South, New York, N.Y. 10016. Residents of New York, New Jersey and Pennsylvania must include sales tax. DO NOT SEND CASH.